W9-BFT-828

THE LAST ANALYSIS

Also by Saul Bellow

HERZOG

HENDERSON THE RAIN KING

SEIZE THE DAY

THE ADVENTURES OF AUGIE MARCH

THE VICTIM

DANGLING MAN

THE
LAST
ANALYSIS

a play by

SAUL
BELLOW

New York · The Viking Press

Copyright © 1962, 1965 by Saul Bellow
All rights reserved

COMPASS BOOKS EDITION
Issued in 1966 by The Viking Press, Inc.
625 Madison Avenue, New York, N.Y. 10022

Published simultaneously in Canada by
The Macmillan Company of Canada Limited

Printed in U.S.A.

Portions of this play were first published, in somewhat different form,
in *Partisan Review*.

This play in its printed form is designed for the reading public only.
All dramatic rights in it are fully protected by copyright, and no
public or private performance—professional or amateur—may be
given without the written permission of the author and the payment
of royalty. As the courts have also ruled that the public reading of a
play constitutes a public performance, no such reading may be given
except under the conditions stated above. Anyone disregarding the
author's rights renders himself liable to prosecution. Communications
regarding these rights should be addressed to the author's representa-
tive, Toby Cole, 234 West 44th Street, New York, N.Y. 10036.

To my son Adam, who had

a great time in the Belasco Theatre

Author's Note

An earlier version of *The Last Analysis,* produced by Roger
Stevens, directed by Joseph Anthony, with Sam Levene,
Tresa Hughes, Leon Janney, and Lucille Patton in the prin-
cipal roles, opened at the Belasco Theatre, New York City,
in September 1964, and closed after a short run. The present
version makes use of some of the timbers of that shipwreck,
but much of it is entirely new. I have dropped several characters, written one new part, attempted to simplify the cluttered and inconsequent plot, which puzzled the audience
(and even the playwright), and tried to eliminate pointless
noises and distracting bits of business. I have heard the
Middlebrow defined as one who makes every loss yield a
profit, but at the risk of acquiring a bad name, I feel obliged
to say that a Broadway failure can be an enriching experience. The rehearsals, the previews, the cold and peevish first-
night audience, the judgments of the critics, were of the
greatest value to me.

The Last Analysis is not simply a spoof of Freudian
psychology, though certain analysts have touchily interpreted
it as such. Its real subject is the mind's comical struggle for
survival in an environment of Ideas—its fascination with
metaphors, and the peculiarly literal and solemn manner in
which Americans dedicate themselves to programs, fancies,
or brainstorms. In *The Last Analysis* a clown is driven to
thought, and, like modern painters, poets, and musicians
before him, turns into a theoretician. I have always had a
weakness for autodidacts and amateur philosophers and

scientists, and enjoy observing the democratic diffusion of high culture. Regrettably, the Broadway version neglected the *mental* comedy of Bummidge and his family, and I have tried to restore it.

—S.B.

February 1965

Cast of Characters

BUMMIDGE: A former star whose popularity has declined, now his own psychiatrist. I think of Bummidge as a large man, or at least a stout one. Nearing sixty, he is still eagerly mapping programs and hatching new projects. Half ravaged, half dignified, earnest when he is clowning and clowning when he means to be earnest, he represents the artist who is forced to be his own theoretician. The role requires great subtlety and charm, and extraordinary mimetic powers.

WINKLEMAN: Bummidge's cousin. A lawyer, authoritative and realistic, he has a deep voice, and a slightly oracular style. He has adopted, as Mott points out, the Harvard Club manner.

BELLA: Bummidge's estranged wife. Not as estranged as he would like her to be. Bella is proud of her business-like ways, her air of command. She is an aggressive, hammering woman, large and masculine, elaborately made up and wearing a bottle-green suit trimmed in fox fur, and spike-heeled shoes. She carries a whopping patent-leather purse.

MADGE: Bummidge's sister. The businesswoman, thinly disguised as a Westchester matron.

MAX: Bummidge's son is in his mid-thirties. Impeccably tailored, manicured, barbered, he is nevertheless the Angry Young Man.

AUNT VELMA: Bummidge's ancient aunt and midwife. At the

edge of the grave, and tottering, she is still aggressive. Wears horn-rimmed glasses and smokes cigars.

IMOGEN: Bummidge's secretary. A little darling, the utterly
credulous ingénue. Bummidge's relation to her is
entirely fatherly.

PAMELA: Bummidge's paramour. The relationship has obviously faded. She does not expect to get much more
from him and is tired of humoring him. Her face is
masklike, with raised brows and prim, bland lips. She
has a thin figure and is dressed in a modest suit.

LOUIE MOTT: Bummidge's old pal, the television technician,
is desperately trying to keep youthful. He wears College Shop clothing—a turtle-necked shirt and white
buckskin shoes.

BERTRAM: Bummidge's scientific collaborator, formerly a
ratcatcher. A slender, elderly, terribly smiling man
with high color and false teeth.

GALLUPPO: A private detective. Stocky, shifty, corrupt-look-
ing, he chews a toothpick, at which he occasionally
sniffs furtively.

AUFSCHNITT: The little Viennese tailor. The part was played
to perfection by Mr. Will Lee at the Belasco Theatre.

FIDDLEMAN: An impresario. He wears a colored vest, has
ducal grand manners in the Hollywood style, and
speaks very impatiently.

A TECHNICIAN

A MESSENGER

ACT ONE

A two-story loft in a warehouse on the West Side of New York, brightly lighted by a studio window. Upstage left, a door to the fire escape. There are also exits to the library, stage right, and through an old-fashioned fire door, stage left. At the back of stage right is a little iron staircase leading to a small balcony. The bathroom door is at stage left. Characters arriving from the street enter through an elevator door, stage right.

The stage is not cluttered. It is hung with bright fabrics, though they are by no means new. The inhabitant of this loft is obviously eccentric. He keeps an old barber chair, downstage right, and an elegant old sofa such as an analyst of the Vienna school might have used, downstage left. The posters on the wall go back to the twenties and thirties— BUMMY, THE OLD TRILBY THEATRE. ZANY BUMMIDGE OF THE FOLLIES. KING OF THE CLOWNS. BUMMY WE LOVE YOU. *Television equipment has been coming in. Obviously, a broadcast is being prepared. There is a floodlamp on the wall, downstage right, in position to cover the barber chair. Near the sofa is a bust of Sigmund Freud. Behind it, bookcases with learned-looking tomes and journals. In center stage is a movable platform.*

At curtain, we discover Bummidge lying in the barber chair, completely covered by a sheet. Imogen sits by her desk on a swivel chair, legs crossed, eagerly transcribing notes from a stenographic pad to large file cards. Enter Winkleman.

WINKLEMAN: Imogen, where's my cousin? Oh, there. Now, Bummy—

IMOGEN: Please, Lawyer Winkleman. I just got him to rest. The strain of today's broadcast is twisting his nerves.

WINKLEMAN, *looking about*: Ah, television equipment. But not the real thing. Only closed-circuit. There was a time when my cousin Bummidge was king of the networks—the greatest comedian of his time. Now look at him, almost destroyed by his ideas, mental experiments—home-brewed psychoanalysis. Poor has-been.

Bummidge quivers under the sheet.

He spends his days in an old loft with his colleagues—*a gesture at Imogen*—acting out his neuroses. His traumas. The psychological crises of his life. It's very painful.

IMOGEN: It's almost deliberate, Mr. Winkleman, the way you refuse to understand.

WINKLEMAN: What's to understand?

BUMMIDGE—*tears off the sheet*: Don't waste your time, Imogen. He pretends to be a genuine lowbrow, a plebeian. *You* know, Winkie, why I act out my past life.

WINKLEMAN, *with heavy irony*: Yeah, self-knowledge.

BUMMIDGE: If a man like me needs insight, why should he go to some punk? I have my own method—*Existenz*-Action-Self-analysis.

WINKLEMAN: Once you were in a class with Bert Lahr, Groucho Marx. Now I foresee you waiting in an alley for a handout of dried eggs from Federal Surplus.

IMOGEN, *to Bummidge*: Finish your rest. You have to have it.

WINKLEMAN: Lowbrow! For you no brow could ever be high enough. Some people are social climbers. You are a mental climber. I'm not against thought, but you're a comic, not a scientist. Is this a time to plunge into theory? Originality? Delirium! And now, with a secretary who used to be a bunny in the Playboy Club, and a collaborator who used to be a ratcatcher . . . now you spend your last dough on a closed-circuit TV broadcast to a bunch of specialists at the American Psychiatric Association. How was it arranged? Whom did you bribe on the Program Committee?

BUMMIDGE, *nettled*: Bribe? They jumped at the chance to see my work.

IMOGEN: Rest . . . I don't know how his organism stands the strain. *She draws the sheet over him.*

WINKLEMAN: And whose equipment is this? *Reads label.* Diamond Electronics. I thought so. Louie Mott, your old Hungarian sidekick and errand boy. That swindler. Bummy, listen to me. We have ties. Why, my mother brought you into the world.

BUMMIDGE—*sits up*: Oh, Aunt Velma! That ancient thing, she still exists. She delivered me. She could clue me into the Unconscious in a dozen places. Where is she?

WINKLEMAN: Very busy, in her old age. She said you telephoned her.

IMOGEN: You haven't rested, haven't eaten in two weeks. You must relax a while before you face the cameras.

BUMMIDGE, *as she begins to cover him again*: Today my powers must be at their peak. I must convince everyone.

> *Enter Mott.*

MOTT: Well, my assistant is here. We can hook up the equipment. But first there's one matter to be took up—money, the balance.

Bummidge pulls the sheet over his head.

WINKLEMAN: I knew you'd be mixed up in this, you devious Hungarian. Whenever he's on the brink of disaster, you're always right behind him.

MOTT: Go blow it out, Winkleman. I stood by him for years.

WINKLEMAN: Only because there were broads around.

MOTT: Wink the Fink!

WINKLEMAN: And now this TV racket. I bet you can't transmit to the Waldorf.

MOTT: I could transmit all the way to China, if I wanted. Look at this citation from the College of Surgeons. I filmed the heart operations at Rochester, you ambulance-chaser!

WINKLEMAN: Sex maniac! Deviant!

MOTT: Maybe you fool your pals at the Harvard Club, but not me. I know about your old-peoples'-home racket.

Winkleman flinches.

IMOGEN: Nursing home?

MOTT: You bet. Cousin Winkie bought an old luxury hotel and filled it with ancient, senile old-folks.

WINKLEMAN: Perfectly legitimate. The old Ravenna Towers. Gorgeous! A work of art. The space, the gilt cornices. The doorknobs themselves are priceless.

MOTT: Three bunks to a single room. And your old lady is like the camp commandant.

Winkleman is glaring.

BUMMIDGE: Imogen—tell them to wrangle outside.

MOTT: Bummy, the office insists on the final payment. Five grand.

IMOGEN: What about the thirty-five thousand he already paid you?

MOTT: I can't help it. And no funny stuff, Bummy.

BUMMIDGE—*sits up, the sheet clutched at his throat*: I thought you were pulling with me, Louie. I've invited all those distinguished people. They want to see the results of my research.

MOTT: Okay, fine. But the office . . .

BUMMIDGE, *earnest*: Don't sell out to the bookkeepers. This is of universal significance.

IMOGEN: I'll look for the checkbook.

Bummidge detains her.

BUMMIDGE: Wink. *Beckons him near, speaks sotto voce.* Let me have the dough for a few days.

WINKLEMAN: Cousin, you're joking.

BUMMIDGE: Why joking? I need it. You made millions on me.

WINKLEMAN: Ancient history! That was when you let me do the thinking. I'd like to help. But I have my principles, too, just like you.

BUMMIDGE: O, money! O, Plutus! O, Mammon!

WINKLEMAN: Is anything more horrible than a solemn buffoon. Where are your savings?

BUMMIDGE: In the separation Bella cleaned me out. Two millions.

WINKLEMAN: You made her furious. Your mistresses used her charge accounts.

BUMMIDGE: Don't you know what Freud says about gold? What does the color remind you of?

WINKLEMAN: Try giving Louie here—*gestures*—the other substance. See if he'll take it.

BUMMIDGE: For thirty years you sold me to the lousy public like dry cereal.

WINKLEMAN: Lousy? You lost your touch. They stopped laughing.

BUMMIDGE: I can make those apes laugh any time. At will. *Pause*. It's just that I can't stand the sound they make. And I feel hit by the blast of sickness from their lungs. It makes me shrink.

WINKLEMAN: And you're going to cure the ravaged psyche of the mass. Poor cousin!

BUMMIDGE: You exploited me. Dragged me down into affluence.

MOTT: Let's not forget that check.

IMOGEN, *crossing to desk*: You see me looking for it, don't you?

BUMMIDGE: You made me change my name. Lead a false

life. Maybe an actor must—I'll give you that much. But—
with fervor—now I want insight. Value. I'll die without
value. And finally I've succeeded in getting off the mere
surface of life. Wink, back me today.

WINKLEMAN—*wraps himself in his coat and sits on couch*:
You're not the only one in trouble.

IMOGEN: I came to Mr. Bummidge's door with a question-
naire. Instead of answering my questions, he took me by the
hand and said, "My dear, what do you consider funny?"

MOTT: What did you say?

IMOGEN: I just said, "Me, coming to your door to ask if you
eat soup." And he laughed, and hired me. I believe in him.
Her hand is on her breast. Mr. Winkleman, leading scientists
have agreed to watch. Doctor Gumplovitch, Doctor Ratzenhofer, the giants of American psychiatry. And people from
Princeton and Johns Hopkins, the Ford Foundation. They
know they're dealing with a great artist.

MOTT: I'm waiting!

BUMMIDGE: Calm! *Throws himself back in the chair.*

MOTT: Here's a check. Fill it in. Five zero zero zero and no
one hundred cents.

    Imogen writes.

WINKLEMAN: Between Bella, and his son Max, and his
broads, especially the present one, Pamela, the ex-chorus
girl, I figure he's been taken for ten million. Your sister
Madge and I are worried. Your real friends.

MOTT: Let's have the signature, now.

BUMMIDGE, *as he signs*: Imogen, we must check out a few

things. Where's Bertram? And Kalbfuss! Make sure Kalbfuss will be watching me. Phone his shop.

WINKLEMAN: Kalbfuss? Shop?

Enter a Technician, pushing a television camera.

TECHNICIAN, *to Mott*: Louie, is this the joint? The floor doesn't look solid enough. These boards waggle like loose teeth. *Seeing Imogen*: Well—hello, Miss.

IMOGEN: Bertram went to the Waldorf to see about the canapés and champagne.

WINKLEMAN: Champagne? And who is this Kalbfuss—the lord high egghead? *Speaking to the Technician and then to Imogen*: Earnestness has been the ruin of my cousin. High-mindedness. The suckers had their mouths open for yucks—he fed them Aristotle, Kierkegaard, Freud. Who needs another homemade intellectual? One more self-nominated boring intellectual, sick with abstractions? An American intellectual?

TECHNICIAN, *pushing equipment before him*: Look out, friend.

WINKLEMAN: Reading! This man hid books in his dressing room. Huge volumes, thick journals. Booksellers were like dope-pushers to him. He was like a junkie—on thought.

IMOGEN: All I can say is that he's done great things for my mental development. He saw more than these externals. No other man has ever been willing to look past them.

The Technician whistles at her.

MOTT, *sniffing her*: She's like a mound of nectarines— Business first. I'll run down to the bank. *Exit.*

BUMMIDGE: Oh! *Sits up*. The time is short. I've got so much mental preparation to make, and I'm hampered, hindered, held back, obstructed, impeded, impaired. *To Winkleman*: Where is your mother? I need those sagging bones. I want her here today. *Crossing stage*: And Bertram—Kalbfuss. He's crucial. Come, Imogen. *Exit stage right*.

    As Imogen follows, the Technician pinches her.

IMOGEN: Yes, Mr. Bummidge. *To Technician*: Please! *Exit*.

WINKLEMAN: No matter what Bummy masterminded, no matter what he brewed, I could make use of it. It brought me a buck, and a tax-clean buck, too. With phantasmagoria like his there's only one thing to do: sell them! When he wanted to weave rugs, I put him into a Fifth Avenue window. If he wanted to paint action pictures, play the organ like Albert Schweitzer, I'd make a deal. But now he's lost his image with the public, he's confused the Plain Man, and that's the sonofabitch that pays for the whole show. . . . I admit I also have a bad character. It's true, I no longer care who lives and who dies. Still, I have to pursue my own way. It's a job, and jobs have to be done. And I'm in trouble myself. He's not the only one. *Moves upstage and right*. He doesn't know it yet, but he's going to save the day for me, as he's done before. Keep sharp, look sharp, Winkie. Lurk offshore. Rush in at the right moment and grab Bummy again. Hide, wait, listen, haunt the fringes, you'll get benefits. And now, a little oxygen for the system—*inhales*—and submerge. *Exit, holding his nose like a swimmer*.

    Enter Bummidge with a timer.

BUMMIDGE: Hours and minutes! No time. Curse that interfering Winkleman. I know he wants to exploit me. He and my sister Madge, they always work together. There's some intrigue. *He wipes them away with a gesture.* Now I am alone. *Puts the timer on the platform, center.* Ultimate reality—that's what we want. Deep, deep and final. The truth which daily life only distorts. Okay, Bummy. *Sits on platform.* What's on your mind? Come, boy, let's have it. Begin with the dreams you dreamt last night. Sleep is dotted with madness. Each dream is a tiny psychosis. The sleeper is a tranquil criminal. All right—the dreams. . . . What I dreamt! A huge white animal climbed into my bed. I thought, "A polar bear." I looked again and saw pig's feet. A white sow. But wait—I didn't do anything to her. A nursing pig. What's the symbolism of it? *Ponders, then shrugs.* I thought, "Live and let live. Let her lie there." I moved over on the diagonal. Part of my basic submissiveness. At least I didn't have to make love to her. But the dream, the dream! The pig squirmed and writhed like a phantom knockwurst, and turned into a fat, enormous man in a baggy sweater with little candy milk bottles sewn in rows. Like Hermann Goering with his medals. But was this fat man a man? In the unconscious, to be obese is female. Oh, that unconscious! Is it ever cunning! Repression! The power of the Id! This was a male with breasts. *Rises.* I want notes on this, for the record. *Calls:* Imogen! Is that girl slipping, libido-wise? Wait, there's more. *Crosses over and sits on his analytic sofa.* Then he/she lay in bed with me, shaking, and all the little bottles clinked and jingled. He/she was laughing. *Laughs in several keys, assuming various characters:* He-he-he! Ha! Hoo-hoo-hoo! That laughter! *Now he is grave.* A nightmare. The creature mocked me. I'm afraid I may not be taken seriously in the field of science. And I no longer know what laughter is. I've lost my bearings and it all sounds wrong to me. In the dream I threw a fit. I puffed up with rage like a squid. My psyche let out angry ink. I almost levitated from the bed. And I cried out in many tongues—"*Nefesh, Ish. Ecce homo. Ho thanatos,*" in Hebrew, Latin, Greek, and bared my chest in the dead eye of the floating moon. Seen through the skylight. And . . . *He staggers a bit.*

> *Enter Imogen, with the Technician close behind her.*

IMOGEN: Please! You must let me alone!

BUMMIDGE: Imogen, is this one of your sexual lapses?

IMOGEN: Of course not, Mr. Bummidge.

BUMMIDGE, *to the Technician*: I'm going to request that you leave this broad alone.

TECHNICIAN: *I*, let *her* alone? *Laughs.* Do I wear lipstick, use perfume, waggle my behind? *She* does it.

BUMMIDGE: Such random eroticism is a bad sign. Is your home life so inadequate that you become inflamed before dinner? *The Technician laughs. Bummidge is enraged.* Listen to that laugh. Is that neurotic, or is that neurotic? Boy, what decadence! Malignancy in the marrow of society. *Sits in barber chair.*

TECHNICIAN, *to Imogen*: Is he serious? *Laughs.* Is that Bummidge the comedian? He's lost his marbles. *Exit.*

BUMMIDGE: You'd better adjust yourself a bit.

> *Imogen turns her back to Bummidge. He buttons her dress.*

IMOGEN: It makes me so unhappy. I try to communicate with people, but they only pay attention to my body.

BUMMIDGE, *sympathetic*: Ah, yes.

IMOGEN—*sits on his knee, filially*: That's why I understand when you try to speak seriously, and they insist on treating you like a hambone comedian. They don't know how profound you are.

BUMMIDGE—*he has picked up a hand mirror and is grimacing into it*: I look frightful. Can people accept my message of sanity and health if I look like death or madness?

IMOGEN: But you're making faces before you look.

BUMMIDGE, *to the mirror*: Come on, you! I know your lousy tricks! Humankind must tear itself away from its nonsense.

IMOGEN: I just know you'll win today. It's bound to be a triumph. I feel it.

BUMMIDGE, *eager*: You think so? Thank you, Imogen. You help me bear my burden. What time is it?

IMOGEN: Two-oh-nine.

Both rise quickly.

BUMMIDGE: Even time is my enemy today. *Crosses stage.* I haven't decided on an opening for my TV appearance. What music shall we begin with?

IMOGEN, *looking through records*: Well, we have Wagner, Grieg, and here's "Les Sylphidees."

BUMMIDGE—*stands beside bust of Freud*: Where shall I stand? Here? Maybe with this bust of Freud. Just the two of us. I'll wear a special coat I designed. Aufschnitt is bringing it. He'll want money too.

IMOGEN: Here's classical guitar music.

BUMMIDGE: No, something wilder. Music to denote that I've roused the sleeping Titans of the instincts. Wham! Crash! Thunder! Remember who'll be watching at the Waldorf. I've invited not only psychologists and analysts, but artists, too, and comedians. I want the comedians to see how the analysts laugh. I want the analysts to see how seriously the comedians take me. I must reach everyone. Everything. Heart, reason, comic spirit. I have something tremendous to say. I want to persuade them. Move them. Stun them . . . Oh, Imogen, I'm frightened. My fingers are freezing.

IMOGEN—*chafing his hands*: You'll do it.

> *She begins to drape the barber chair with tapestries.*

BUMMIDGE: The enterprise is bigger than me, but there's nobody else to do it. What are these fabrics?

IMOGEN: For a papal-throne effect.

BUMMIDGE: I've also invited the clergy. Where is Bertram? Louie—at the bank with my bad check. I must raise the money. Meantime, my schedule. My inner self. Oh-oh—my sordid sister.

> *Exit Imogen, as Madge enters. Madge is conservatively dressed; the matron from New Rochelle is what she tries to be.*

MADGE: Well, Bummy, what's all the excitement?

BUMMIDGE, *at first trying to charm her*: Madge, dear, what a surprise! But I knew you'd come.

MADGE: Naturally. You were weeping on the phone. I thought you were dying. How nice to see TV equipment again. A reminder of your former greatness.

BUMMIDGE—*more charm*: Madge, I've missed you. You have Mama's sense of humor.

MADGE: The good old days! The big time, the celebrities, the beautiful trips. I'm often sorry for you, Philip.

BUMMIDGE: You think I goofed.

MADGE: Are you as prosperous in psychoanalysis as you were in show business?

BUMMIDGE: How's Harold?

MADGE, *indifferently*: The same.

    They kiss.

BUMMIDGE: Madge, I need five thousand dollars.

MADGE—*laughs*: Oh, Bummy!

BUMMIDGE—*behaves oddly when she laughs; puts his ear to her chest like a physician*: That makes you laugh? Laugh again.

MADGE, *pushing him off*: First you read these books, then you turn into a mad scientist. You have to broadcast your message on closed-circuit. . . .

BUMMIDGE: Any minute, Louie Mott will be back from the bank with a bad check.

MADGE: You're putting me on. It's just your idiosyncrasy to live in this warehouse and play psychologist with a dumb doll and a ratcatcher. You didn't let Max and Bella and Pamela take *everything*!

BUMMIDGE: Why leave yourself off the list? Madge, we're siblings. Sib-lings! From the same womb. It's not like being registered in the same hotel, different nights.

MADGE: I'm grateful to you for what little I have. But don't forget *my* problems. Why, Harold alone—first his prostate, then his coronary, then his eyes!

BUMMIDGE: I wish I were a modest failure like Harold—no broad perspectives, no ideas, adrift with bifocals. All I'm asking is five—

MADGE—*laughs*: Peanuts, to a former millionaire.

BUMMIDGE: Your laughter fascinates me. Mama had a throaty laugh. Yours has little screams and cries in it. *Imitates.* But don't make a poor mouth. *Seizes her wrist.* You took your diamonds off in the street. I can see the marks.

MADGE—*jerks away her arm*: Your sister will show you how broke she is. My very slip is torn. *She shows the lace of her slip; it hangs loose.*

BUMMIDGE, *voice rising*: Oh, my Lord! Your underwear. *Fingers it.* Your underwear!

MADGE: Now even you can understand how it is.

BUMMIDGE: Wait! What's happening. My unconscious is trying to tell me something. What, you primitive devil—guilt? Lust? Crime? Tell me! *Prods his head.*

MADGE: I hope you're satisfied.

BUMMIDGE: I hear the groaning past—like a bass fiddle. *He makes deep sounds in his throat.* Madge, you've mobilized ancient emotions.

MADGE: I can't stay.

BUMMIDGE—*clinging to the lace*: Wait!

    They both tug.

MADGE: Let go my slip.

BUMMIDGE: Answer some questions about Williamsburg, where we lived behind the store.

MADGE: Hideous place. I was ashamed to bring a boy to the house.

BUMMIDGE: The scene of my infancy.

MADGE: So, put up a plaque—you're tearing my clothing, Bummy.

BUMMIDGE, *now on his knees*: I'm on an expedition to recover the forgotten truth. Madge, you have no idea what human beings really are; the stages of the psyche—polymorphous, oral, anal, narcissistic. It's fantastic, intricate, complicated, hidden. How can you live without knowing? Madge, look deep! Infinite and deep!

MADGE: You want me to be as confused as yourself? Get out from under my skirt. Freud is passé. Even I know it. *Rises in haste.*

BUMMIDGE, *tearing the lace from her slip*: I need this. *Puts it to his nose.*

MADGE: You're stripping me!

BUMMIDGE—*rises*: It's coming back to me. Ah! A sealed door has burst open. Dusty light is pouring out. Madge—Madge!

MADGE: I'm leaving.

BUMMIDGE—*stops her*: No. You have to share this with me—this trauma you gave me at eleven. You caught me fooling with the things in your dresser. We'll re-enact it. Eleven and thirteen. You catch me. Scream for Mama.

MADGE: No, I won't.

BUMMIDGE—*stamps his foot*: You will. You owe it to me. You damaged me. *Changing tone*: It'll do you good, too.

MADGE: It's crazy. Twenty-four hours a day, I have to defend myself from insanity.

BUMMIDGE, *leading her to his desk*: This is the dresser. You surprise me as I fondle your step-ins. Clutch my arm and shout *Mama, Mama!*

> *During the following action, Max, Imogen, Bertram, and Winkleman enter and watch. Bummidge in pantomime opens a drawer and feels silks with adolescent lasciviousness. Madge falls on him from behind with a sudden cry.*

MADGE: Mama! Mama!

BUMMIDGE: That's not right. Give it more. Again, and use your nails, too.

MADGE: Mama!

BUMMIDGE: You're beginning to have that bitchy tone I remember. But more.

MADGE—*piercing*: Ma!

BUMMIDGE: More yet. *Pinches her.*

MADGE, *fiercely*: You nasty, sneaking little bastard.

BUMMIDGE, *triumphant*: The old Madge. You can hear it yourself.

MADGE, *inspired*: Look what I caught him doing, Mama. I'm the daughter, the only daughter, and I have no privacy in this filthy, foul, horrible hole. Look what I caught him doing.

He'll end up with the whores yet. Dirty, snotty, cockeyed little poolroom bum!

BUMMIDGE, *squatting*: Right—right! And I crouch there, trapped, quivering, delight turning to horror. I'm the human Thing—the peculiar beast that feels shame. And now Mama's swinging at me.

> *He ducks. Madge swipes at him with a broom.*

Don't hit me.

MADGE, *shaken*: Who *am* I, anyway?

WINKLEMAN: If this isn't spooky. Playing with dead relatives.

MAX, *angry*: Hey, what about a minute for a living relative? It's me, your son, your only child. Remember? You damn well will. I'll see to that.

BUMMIDGE: One generation at a time. Bertram, did you see this?

BERTRAM: I sure did. You're all shook up.

BUMMIDGE: A petticoat. Lace. Hem. I was hemmed in. A boy's awakening sex cruelly suppressed. A drawer. Drawer—coffin—death. Poor things that we are. Binding with briars the joys and desires. Madge, you see how I work?

MADGE—*matronly composure beginning to return*: Ridiculous!

MAX: That's what I say. A crude joke.

BUMMIDGE—*turns to him*: Can you tell me what a joke is? *He starts to leave.*

MAX: Stay here. Once and for all, we're going to have it out.

BUMMIDGE: Come, Bert—Imogen. Help . . . upstairs. Consultation . . .

MAX: Pop, I warn you. . . .

IMOGEN: An artist like your father is entitled to respect.

MAX: Artist? Feet of clay, all the way up to the ears.

BUMMIDGE: Wink. Your mother. Tante Velma. Bring her.

> *Exit with Imogen and Bertram, smelling Madge's lace.*

WINKLEMAN: Would anyone pay to see him carry on like this?

MAX: An obsolete comedian? His generation is dead. Good riddance to that square old stuff. . . . What are you doing here, Winkie—you want to con something out of him?

WINKLEMAN: How delightful to hear a youthful point of view.

MAX, *to Madge*: And what's your angle? You didn't come to give him a glass of Yiddisher tea.

MADGE: I'm his agent still. And Wink's his lawyer.

MAX: Parasites, germs and viruses. You two, and Pamela, the famous Southern choreographer . . .

MADGE: You went through quite a chunk of money yourself. Well, your mother took Bummy's millions; what do you want with him?

MAX: Yesterday my old man raised thirty-five thousand on the property in Staten Island. It's mine in trust. He's spending it on this TV production. . . . Pathetic show-off slob. But I'm going to stop him.

Exit angry and determined.

WINKLEMAN: What's he up to? He probably owes his bookie. He's forever in a booth having long phone conversations with crooks. Dimes are like goof pills to him. I'm glad I never had a son, never married.

MADGE: Why didn't you?

WINKLEMAN: I know my married friends lead *lovely* lives. But me? *An elaborate sigh, mocking himself and Madge*: There's an old poem—
> To hold a horse, you need a rein,
> To hold an elephant, a chain,
> To hold a woman, you need a heart. . . .

MADGE: Everyone has a heart.

WINKLEMAN: Every restaurant serves potatoes. *Pause.* We served too many potatoes to the old people. Now we're in trouble.

MADGE: Does Bummy suspect anything?

WINKLEMAN: So far I've kept it out of the news. Eight cases of malnutrition. If the inspector breaks it to the papers we're ruined. I socked a quarter of a million into this. I told you we couldn't feed 'em on a buck a day.

MADGE: We could, but your mother took kickbacks on meat, eggs, bread, milk. Face it, she starved them.

WINKLEMAN—*opens a newspaper*: You gave her a hopeless budget. Look at these prices. Pot roast sixty-eight cents. Ground meat forty-three cents. And what about special diets? Some of these people have diabetes, anemia.

MADGE: Why waste time here? I know, we need a lump of

money to bribe our way out of a scandal. *Pause.* Only think, we used to get half a million a year out of Bummy. But that was before he shot his bolt.

WINKLEMAN: Still, he's never lost his audience sense.

MADGE: He did. He turned solemn, boring, a Dutch uncle, a scold.

WINKLEMAN: Scolding is a career too. Some of our biggest idealists made a fortune, scolding.

MADGE: He should have stuck to his nonsense.

WINKLEMAN: But that's just it. The great public is tired of the old nonsense-type nonsense. It's ready for serious-type nonsense. This psychological set-up is just the thing for a comeback. I would have given him the five thousand.

MADGE: Are you out of your head? Today? When we need every penny?

WINKLEMAN: I still say cooperate. I don't know what those highbrows at the Waldorf will think of his shenanigans, but what would Madison Ave. think?

MADGE, *pondering*: You always were a thoughtful, imaginative angler.

WINKLEMAN—*bows, acknowledging the compliment*: I've been in touch with Fiddleman.

MADGE, *thunderstruck*: Fiddleman! But he wrote Bummy off years ago.

WINKLEMAN: At this moment, Fiddleman, kingpin impresario, bigger than Hurok, is in his limousine en route to the Waldorf to watch the telecast at my invitation. Don't forget, those people are up against it for novelty. A billion-dollar industry, desperate for innovation. It fears death. It has to come up with something big, original, every month.

MADGE: Maybe. But would Bummy go commercial again? He's half nuts over Freud. Just as Freud becomes old hat.

WINKLEMAN: But on the lower levels the social order is just catching up with psychoanalysis. The masses want their share of insight. Anyway, put a five-million-dollar contract under Bummy's nose, and see what happens.

MADGE: Five! My commission is ten per cent. . . . Winkie, I'm sure he still has money stashed away. In this joint, too.

WINKLEMAN: Crafty he's always been.

MADGE: He'd never hide it. He always loved "The Purloined Letter." He'd put his dough in an obvious place. For instance, what's this old valise?

WINKLEMAN: Open it.

MADGE: It's locked. Chained to this barber chair.

WINKLEMAN: He's his own bag man. This is his loot.

MADGE: Tip the chair, and I'll slip the chain out.

WINKLEMAN: Theft? Me? I'm a lawyer. I may be disbarred as it is.

MADGE: Calling me poor-mouth.

WINKLEMAN: Reading me sermons on anality. Ha-ha! That nut. He has charm. You must admit it.

Shouting is heard above.

My ridiculous cousin. What's he yelling about?

MADGE: Let's have a talk.

They go. Enter Bertram and Imogen, supporting Bummidge.

BERTRAM: Lucky I heard you. You almost fell out of the window.

IMOGEN: Why did you lean out so far?

BUMMIDGE: I saw Louie coming from the bank. Bertram, stall him. Keep the equipment coming.

BERTRAM: I'll do what I can. *Exit.*

BUMMIDGE, *calling after Bertram*: Bring me a sandwich. Imogen, where's the schedule? *Reads schedule.* Dreams. Madge. Aunt Velma. Couch work. I haven't done the couch work. Before the broadcast, I must. There's still a big block. *Brings out a screen and places it at the head of the couch.*

IMOGEN: You haven't eaten, haven't shaved.

BUMMIDGE: I can't stop. Must barrel through. This may be one of those central occasions in the history of civilization. I claim nothing personally. I'm the instrument of a purpose beyond ordinary purpose. I may be the only man on the Eastern Seaboard with a definitely higher purpose. What a thing to get stuck with!

IMOGEN: Ready for the session. *Sits with stenographic pad.* Number eight-one-oh-eight.

BUMMIDGE, *lying down*: Eight-one-oh-eight. *Mutters*: One-oh-eight. *Rises*. Imogen, I can't do this alone. I must call in the analyst.

IMOGEN: I understand. The tension must be frightful.

BUMMIDGE—*goes behind the screen and emerges as the analyst, in horn-rimmed smoked glasses*: Well, Mr. Bummidge, how is the psyche today? Lie down, stretch out. How do you intend to proceed? I leave you complete freedom of choice, as an analyst should.

> *Throughout this scene, he wears glasses as the analyst. Removing them, he is the patient.*

BUMMIDGE (PATIENT): Doctor, things are not good. Last night I dreamed of a male with breasts. After this I found myself in a swimming pool, not swimming, not wet. An old gentleman with a long beard floats by. Such a long white beard, and rosy cheeks.

BUMMIDGE (ANALYST): The material is quite mixed. Water stands for the amniotic bag-of-waters. A beard refers to the father-figure.

BUMMIDGE (PATIENT): I have to tell you, Doctor, I'm fed up with these boring figures in my unconscious. It's always Father, Mother. Or again, breast, castration, anxiety, fixation to the past. I am desperately bored with these things, sick of them!

BUMMIDGE (ANALYST): You're sick *from* them. Of course. We are all sick. That is our condition. Man is the sick animal. Repression is the root of his madness, and also of his achievements.

BUMMIDGE (PATIENT): Oh, Doctor, why can't I live without hope, like everybody else?

BUMMIDGE (ANALYST): Mr. Bummidge, you are timid but obstinate. Exceptional but commonplace. Amusing but sad. A coward but brave. You are stuck. The Id will not release you to the Ego, and the Ego cannot let you go to the Id.

BUMMIDGE (PATIENT): No resolution?

BUMMIDGE (ANALYST): Perhaps. If you can laugh. But face the void of death. Why do you dream of your father?

BUMMIDGE (PATIENT): But was it Papa? Papa had no beard. In his last illness, he shaved his mustache. *Sits.* I was shocked by this. Pa . . . oh, Pa, your lip is so white. Age and weakness have suddenly come over you. Too feeble to count out the *Daily Mirrors.* Mustache gone, face changed, your eyes are so flat, they show death. Death, what are you doing to Papa? You can't . . . Is this the mighty hero I feared? Him with the white lip? Papa, don't go from us.

BUMMIDGE (ANALYST): Don't be deceived by surface feelings, Mr. Bummidge. Remember—ambivalence. You may not really feel compassion. An old enemy and rival is going down. In your heart you also exulted. Maybe you wanted him to live only to see your success.

BUMMIDGE (PATIENT): I don't believe it.

IMOGEN—*applauding*: Good!

BUMMIDGE (PATIENT): You're a hard-nosed man. Why do you prefer the ugliest interpretations? Why do you pollute all my good impulses?

Enter Bertram with a sandwich.

I loved my old father. . . . I want to weep.

IMOGEN: He's giving it to himself today.

BUMMIDGE (ANALYST): Did I invent the human species? It can't be helped. I want to cry, too.

BUMMIDGE (PATIENT): My father couldn't bear the sight of me. I had adenoids, my mouth hung open—was that a thing to beat me for? I liked to hum to myself while eating—was that a thing to beat me for? I loved to read the funnies—is that any reason to whip a child? *Looks into sandwich and mutters to Bertram*: More mustard. *His voice rises*: Killjoy! A human life was in my breast, you old killjoy. You attacked all my pleasure sources. But I fought. I hid in the cellar. I forged your signature on my report card. I ate pork. I was a headliner at the good old Trilby. The good-for-nothing became a star and earned millions, making people laugh—all but Papa. He never laughed. What a peevish face. Laugh, you old Turk. Never! Censure. Always censure. Well, you grim old bastard, I made it. You're dead, and I'm still jumping. What do I care for your grave? Let Madge look after it. Down goes the coffin. Down. The hole fills with clay. But Bummidge is still spilling gravy at life's banquet, and out front they're laughing fit to bust. *He laughs, close to tears*. Yes, I am that crass man, Bummidge. Oh, how foul my soul is! I have the Pagliacci gangrene. Ha, ha, ha—weep, weep, weep! *Buries his face in his hands*.

BUMMIDGE (ANALYST): Do you see the Oedipal strain in this situation? What of your mother?

BUMMIDGE (PATIENT): I saw I'd have Mama to myself. *She* laughed. Oh what a fat throaty laugh she had. Her apron shook.

BUMMIDGE (ANALYST): But what did you want with your mother?

BUMMIDGE (PATIENT): You mean the mother who bathed me in the little tin tub by the kitchen stove? Oh, Doctor, what are you suggesting?

BUMMIDGE (ANALYST): Don't repress the poisonous truth. Go deeper.

BUMMIDGE (PATIENT): How deep?

BUMMIDGE (ANALYST): As deep as you can.

BUMMIDGE (PATIENT): Will there ever be a bottom?

BUMMIDGE (ANALYST): Does the universe have a bottom?

BUMMIDGE (PATIENT): How can I bear it? I, too, am blind. Like Oedipus, far gone in corrupt habits. Oh, hubris! I put a rose bush on Mama's grave. But Papa's grave is sinking, sinking. Weeds cover the tombstone. Oh, shame, Jocasta! *Collapses on the sofa.*

IMOGEN: Oh, Mr. Bummidge, marvelous!

BERTRAM: Quite extraordinary. If you perform like this on television, the analysts will give you an ovation.

IMOGEN: He ought to have the Nobel Prize. I think psychology is worth every sacrifice. I love it more and more.

BUMMIDGE: My whole brain is like a sea of light. *He unlocks the valise. Now Bummidge the patient puts twenty dollars on the chair.* This is one point on which I can't break with orthodox Freudianism. You must pay the analyst.

    Enter Madge.

MADGE: What is this?

BUMMIDGE (ANALYST)—*picks up the money*: Thank you.

BERTRAM: Better lock up the doctor's money.

IMOGEN: Bank it for him.

BUMMIDGE: He prefers it this way.

    Exit Bummidge, with Bertram and Imogen.

MADGE, *going rapidly to the bag*: Money. Loaded.

Enter Mott.

MOTT, *angry, shaken*: Boy, is he dishonest! Bummy! Where is he, your brother? He wrote a bad check.

MADGE: Oh, the poor kid. Stalling for a little time.

MOTT: I wouldn't believe the teller. No funds! "What?" I said—Bummy complains there are no more real underlings. Just bureaucrats, full of aggression.

MADGE, *soothing*: You won't pull out because of a few dollars. This broadcast is too important, Louie.

MOTT: No sweet talk, please. It's too late. Thirty years ago you turned me down flat.

MADGE—*shades of youthful allure*: I was a foolish girl. I thought you were attacking me. I'd be smarter now, maybe. You're still so youthful.

MOTT: Excuse me. . . . I didn't mean . . . I think you're lovely. Don't get me wrong. . . . I used to get such a flash when I saw you—in the old days.

MADGE, *with, alas, antiquated wiles*: You're a dear, Louie. Louie, we mustn't let my brother down. He's been a true friend. He saved you from those Boston hoodlums during Prohibition.

MOTT: True. I was in the dehydrated-wine business. Dry, purple bricks. Add water, make wine. Boston Blackie tried to muscle me out.

MADGE: Bummy saved you.

MOTT: Yes, true. I don't deny it. I tell everybody. But . . .

MADGE: He's always helped you. Staked you six different times. Covered for you with women. Even got you this little electronics racket.

MOTT: I admit that. He paid for the course. Enrolled me personally.

MADGE: Don't cry. I know how emotion tears your Hungarian heart.

MOTT, *moved*: Bummy says I suffer from moral dizziness. No roots. Only loose wires. It's all true. But when he gives bad checks . . .

MADGE: Louie, I myself will make it good.

MOTT: You? *All business again*: Sorry . . . but not in trade. I have to have cash.

MADGE, *stung*: Don't be nasty! *Recovers*. Old friend, I'll let you in on a good thing. We have people watching at the Waldorf. Fiddleman . . .

MOTT, *impressed*: Leslie—the impresario?

MADGE: You know my brother still has greatness in him. He's due for a revival. He'll be bigger than ever. I want you to pipe the performance not only to the scientists but also to an adjoining suite. NBC, CBS, MCA will be watching. With sponsors. The biggest.

MOTT: Is that so? That's clever. Can do. But the money . . .

MADGE: You'll be cut in. There's money for all. I guarantee it. *She lightly kicks Bummidge's bag*. You want it in black and white?

Enter Technician.

TECHNICIAN: Well, what gives?

MOTT—*wavers, then decides*: We work. Start hooking up.

> *Madge and Mott shake hands. Exit Madge, right.*
> *Enter Bummidge, now wearing trousers and a T*
> *shirt. Max follows him.*

BUMMIDGE: Max, don't be destructive.

MAX: Take this crap out.

BUMMIDGE: Oh, Louie. Don't let me down over a few bucks.
I know the check was rubber, but—

MOTT: It was a lousy thing to do. But I've thought it over
and decided to do the big thing. You have another hour to
raise the dough.

BUMMIDGE, *sincerely grateful*: Oh, you generous heart.

MAX, *seizing a cable*: You won't squander my inheritance.

> *He and Bummidge and Mott tug at cable.*

TECHNICIAN: That line is hot. Watch it!

> *The fuses blow. The stage is plunged into darkness.*
> *Green and red sparks fly. Bummidge screams.*

BUMMIDGE: My son wants to electrocute me!

MOTT: He blew everything.

BUMMIDGE: Ruined! Lights, lights! Imogen! Bertram!

MOTT: My flashlight! We have to find the fusebox.

> *Bummidge lights a candle, Mott holding a flashlight.*
> *Mott and Technician run out.*

BUMMIDGE: What the Christ do you think you're doing?

MAX: You're not throwing my dough out the window. I need it today. And the hell with your originality.

BUMMIDGE: Every moment is precious. Guests are waiting at the Waldorf—eminent people.

MAX: Sure, you're the center of everything. Everybody has to wait. You breathe all the air, eat all the food, and lay all the women.

BUMMIDGE—*alters his tone*: Poor child, master this Oedipal hate and love. You're no kid. You mustn't waste fifty years distorting simple facts. Your father is only flesh and blood. Reason is your only help. Think, Max, think for dear life.

MAX: You think. Why wouldn't you be Bella's husband, the public's favorite?

BUMMIDGE: You mean a nice, square, chuckling Santa Claus to entertain the expense-account aristocracy with gags.

MAX: What else are you good for?

BUMMIDGE: I'm all for the emancipation of youth. Even at your age. Fight with authority, yes. But what good is that doggish look, that cool, heavy, sullen expression? My boy, this war of fathers and sons is a racket. Humankind has a horrible instinct for complaint. It's one whole section of the death instinct.

MAX: If we're going to have one of these high-level theoretical talks, you might start by zipping your fly.

BUMMIDGE: Is it open? It isn't worth a glance.

MAX: Showoff! You want to be the great stud. And I'm just a sample of your marvelous work.

BUMMIDGE: Not true. You're still just one of these child fanatics.

MAX: You made me drive you and that choreographer to Boston on *business*. Well, she was giving me the high sign.

BUMMIDGE: Pamela? Why, you crumb. You—you ex-sperm, you.

MAX: Old egomaniac!

BUMMIDGE: Quick, before you provoke me to terrible violence, what do you want?

MAX: You grabbed my property on Staten Island. That's theft. You owe me a good start in life.

BUMMIDGE: You've had six, seven starts.

MAX, *in earnest*: Come clean with me. What's the reason for this analysis? You latch on to everybody who knocks at the door—delivery boys, ratcatchers, bill collectors. You make them act out psychological situations. Are you kidding your way to God? What makes a comic think he can cure human perversity? It'll only take different forms. If you change your vices, is that progress?

BUMMIDGE: *Only* a comic. Bummidge—he doesn't know Greek or calculus. But he knows what he knows. Have you ever watched audiences laughing? You should see how monstrous it looks; you should listen from my side of the footlights. Oh, the despair, my son! The stale hearts! The snarling and gasping! *He imitates various kinds of laughter—snarling, savage, frightening, howling, quavering*: "Ha, ha—I am a cow, a sheep, a wolf, a rat. I am a victim, a killer. Ha, ha— my soul is corked up forever. Let me out. My spirit is famished. I twist, and rub. Ha, ha, ha, I'm an impostor.

Can't you see? Catch me, please. No, it's too late. Life has no meaning. Ha, ha, ha, ha, ha!"

MAX: Why take it on yourself? Do your work, draw your dough, and to hell with it.

BUMMIDGE: My work? It's being stolen from me. Sophistication is putting me out of business. Everybody is kidding, smiling. Every lie looks like a pleasantry. Destruction appears like horseplay. Chaos is turned into farce, because evil is clever. It knows you can get away with murder if you laugh. Sadism makes fun. Extermination is a riot. And this is what drives clowns to thought. *Gravely*: To thought.

MAX: Why, you have a lump in your throat, Dad.

BUMMIDGE: Max! You called me Dad. Max!

MAX: Pa! *They are about to embrace. He turns.* It's just an expression—don't get all shook up.

BUMMIDGE: But you said it. My son!

MAX: Oh . . . everybody's "Dad."

BUMMIDGE: Except your father.

MAX: Don't confuse everything. I'm here to talk business. Listen, Bummy, there's a shipment of toasters from Czechoslovakia, refused by the importer because the cords are faulty. I know where to put my hands on the right Japanese-made cords, and there's an importer from Honduras, waiting.

BUMMIDGE: What have I begotten?

MAX: Another father would be proud. I beat those Czechs down to nothing. Ten grand today gets me thirty tomorrow. For twenty I can buy into a frozen-lasagne operation. All I want from you is three grand. Deduct it from the thirty-five you stole from me.

BUMMIDGE: In other words, you have seven and need three. Max—*shifting his chair closer confidentially*—why don't you lend me five and take my note for thirty?

MAX, *recoiling*: What, invest in your fantasies?

BUMMIDGE: Me you accuse of fantasy? You with the toasters and the guys from Honduras and Japan who'll make you a fortune in lasagne?

MAX: Is that worse than this giant insanity about psycho-analysis and comedy—this Tower of Babel you're building singlehanded? You think you're a new Moses?

BUMMIDGE: In the sandbox I watched over you. In the incubator I read to you.

MAX: Lucky I couldn't understand. You would have addled my brains, too.

BUMMIDGE: I wanted to lead you out of the realm of projections into the light of sanity. But you prefer the institutionalized psychosis of business.

MAX: Old lunatic!

BUMMIDGE: You may not be my child. Men have been tricked before.

MAX: Profound old fart!

BUMMIDGE: Spirochete! Filterable virus! Go bug your mother!

> *Lights go on.*

MAX: You wait. I'll show you what things are really like. I'll open your eyes about that Pamela broad; I'll plow you.

You hocked my building. *Jumps up and down in a tantrum.*
You could go to jail.

BUMMIDGE: From a winged boy into a tailored vulture.

MAX: I may have you committed. . . . You wait, I'll be back
with a warrant. An injunction. There'll be no telecast. *In
running out he bumps into Mott, Technician, and Bertram.*
Get out of my way! *Exit.*

TECHNICIAN: What's eating him?

BUMMIDGE: My son has wounded me. Wounded me. *Exit.*

MOTT: Tough!

> *He and Technician go about their work. Bertram is
> curious, watching.*

BERTRAM: It all connects, eh? And you'll beam the lecture
to the Waldorf?

MOTT: I could transmit it to Iceland, if I wanted. . . . I
wonder how Bummy'll be.

BERTRAM: Brilliant.

MOTT: Didn't you first come here as the exterminator?

BERTRAM: As soon as I saw the place I realized there were
rats. You ask me how? I feel the molding, the baseboards.
Rats have greasy fur, and they always run along the wall.
Also, a rat drops many pellets.

MOTT: Ugh!

BERTRAM: The expert can date these pellets accurately. By
a gentle squeeze of thumb and forefinger. Infallible. He also
puts an ear to the wall. Rats must gnaw to survive. Otherwise
the fangs'd get too long to chew with, their mouths would

lock, and they'd starve. Bummy and I have scientific interests in common. What now?

TECHNICIAN: We hook the A line to this camera.

BERTRAM: Bummy and I hit it off right away. I got involved in psychotherapy. He showed me that to go around killing rats meant I must be compulsive, obsessional. The rat often symbolizes the child, as in the "Pied Piper." The rat also stands for a primordial mystery. Earth mystery. Chthonic. But most of all, my sense of humor fascinated Bummy. I don't laugh at jokes.

MOTT, *curious*: Never?

BERTRAM: I can't. I'm too neurotic. *He stands between Mott and the Technician.* I have no sense of humor. I only have occasion to laugh.

TECHNICIAN: When does that happen?

BERTRAM: Mainly when I'm tickled.

> *They tickle him. He laughs horribly. They are aghast.*

MOTT: Stop! Stop it!

BERTRAM: I know. It's pathological. Tickling shouldn't make a normal person laugh.

TECHNICIAN: Let's see.

> *He and Mott solemnly tickle each other.*

MOTT: I'm knocking myself out trying to understand about the broadcast. Bummy loves big gestures. Does he want to be a college professor?

> *Enter Imogen.*

IMOGEN: Mr. Bummidge doesn't realize how fast time is passing.

Enter Bummidge.

BUMMIDGE: To understand Max, I must revisit *my* father.

MOTT, *a bit shocked*: But he's dead. . . .

BUMMIDGE: In the unconscious, Louie, there is no time, no logic, and no death.

TECHNICIAN: We need a sound level.

MOTT: I'll set up these lights.

BUMMIDGE: Bertram, you'll play Father. We live behind the candy store in Williamsburg. . . . It was so dark there. Dark. And poverty.

MOTT, *as he works with lights*: Here goes the poor-childhood routine, again. How he fetched wood and coal. Was beaten. Peddled papers. Froze his ears. How there was never real toilet paper in the house, only orange wrappers.

BUMMIDGE: Papa wouldn't allow me to have candy. I stole. I'd wolf down the stale chocolates, choking. Now Bert, as Papa, you discover a Mary Jane wrapper floating in the toilet. You clutch my ear and cry out, "Thief! Goniff!"

BERTRAM, *taking Bummidge by the ear*: Thief—goniff.

IMOGEN: I wouldn't want Bertram to pinch my ear.

BUMMIDGE: Harder, Bert. Don't just squeeze—twist. It's essential to feel the pain.

BERTRAM, *warningly*: It's not a good idea to encourage my cruelty.

MOTT: Go on, Bert, turn it on.

> *Bertram, face transformed, twists. Bummidge screams.*

BUMMIDGE: That's it! Unbearable! *Sinks to his knees.* I haven't felt such agony in forty years. *Supplicating*: Papa, Papa! Don't! I'm only a child. I have an innocent craving for sweets. It's human nature. I inherit it from you. Papa, it's the pleasure principle. Jung and Freud would agree.

IMOGEN: He's read simply everything.

BERTRAM: Mine son stealing?

BUMMIDGE—*rises*: No, Bert, Papa had a ballsy voice. *Imitates his father*: "By thirteen I was already in the sweat shop, brought home pay. God helped, I got this lousy business. All day buried behind a dark counter with broken feet; with gall bladder; blood pressure. I sell egg-cream, mushmellows, cheap cigars, gumballs—all kinds of *dreck*. But you, your head lays in idleness? Play? Fun? Candy? You'll be a *mensch* or I'll kill you." *Himself again*: Desire pierced my glands and my mouth watered. I heard a subversive voice that whispered, "Joy, joy!" It made a criminal of me. *Reflecting*: A humorless savage, he was. But I loved him. Why won't my son love me? My father whipped me. *Bending, he canes himself.*

MOTT: Now he's a flagellant?

BUMMIDGE, *kneeling, head to the floor*: Flogged.

IMOGEN: Oh, dear, he'll have an attack of Humanitis.

TECHNICIAN: What's Humanitis?

BERTRAM: It's when the human condition is suddenly too much for you.

BUMMIDGE, *sitting on floor*: When he punished me, I took myself away and left an empty substitute in his hands. *Crawls toward exit, sits again.* I let myself be punished in effigy. I split up into fragments. There were two, four, an army, and the real Bummidge gets lost. I couldn't keep track. My self got lost. But where is the *me* that is me? What happened to it? *Rises slowly.* That was the beginning of my comic method.

> *Explaining the matter to himself, he goes. Bertram helps him off.*

IMOGEN: We'll never be ready, at this rate.

MOTT, *to Technician*: Run down to the truck and get the rest of those cables.

> *Exit Technician.*

I talked the office into giving Bummy a little more time.

IMOGEN: That's kind of you.

MOTT: That's the kind of friend I am. . . . Imogen. *Takes her hand.* As soon as I saw you, I had like a tremendous flash!

IMOGEN, *trying to free her hand*: Mr. Mott!

MOTT: You're my erotic type.

IMOGEN: Don't, Mr. Mott. I can't bear to be a sexy joke. I really am a serious person.

MOTT: This *is* serious. I'm a mature man, mature and single. Most important, I'm youthful. Most mature men in New

York are married. The rest are queer, crazy, infected, dangerous. But I—

IMOGEN: No, no. Someone's coming. *Flees.*

MOTT: Wait!

> *Exit in pursuit. Enter Pamela. She is, like Madge, highly respectable in appearance, wears a knit suit, a modest hat; she has a slight Southern accent.*

PAMELA: Bummy? Where are you, dear? *Looks for him.* I've come to be with you on this important day. *Seeing she is alone*: It's sure to be a bomb. Then what? Then we can stop pretending. I can't wait. Love, science. "Oh, value, value. I'll die without value." What a drag it's turned into. *Listens.* Footsteps? I'll surprise him.

> *She steps behind the screen. Madge and Winkleman enter.*

WINKLEMAN: It's set, at the Waldorf. The networks, the agencies—Fiddleman. Phew. It took plenty of doing. Fiddleman will phone, the instant the broadcast is over.

MADGE: Bummy's got to get us off the hook. And listen, I saw Bella at Columbus Circle, waiting for a bus. With all her money, she won't take a taxi.

WINKLEMAN: Was she coming here?

MADGE: Where else? What a tough old broad she's become, loud, brassy, suspicious. She'll throw a monkey wrench in the works if she can.

WINKLEMAN: My contact, the inspector, said he'd wait one day. Tomorrow, at the latest, we have to bribe him. Does Bella know we're in a tight spot?

MADGE: She has everyone followed, investigated. She must suspect. How much is that guy holding us up for? . . . I still wonder about this valise of Bummy's. Could I work my hand in? Is it money? Winkie, it is—it is money!

> *Pamela now steps out. Madge's wrist is caught in the valise.*

WINKLEMAN, *trying to cover*: Why, it's Pamela.

PAMELA: Shall we play peek-a-boo? I love to catch people red-handed. Such a luxurious feeling.

MADGE: Help me.

> *With Pamela and Winkleman tugging, Madge frees her hand, and falls backward.*

PAMELA: You'll have to cut me in. Let's not waste time lying. I understand what you're up to. If Bummy gets offers, you'll need my help, my persuasive powers.

MADGE, *as she and Winkleman exchange glances, shrug, accept the inevitable*: Okay.

PAMELA: Life isn't easy for a person like me. If we can put Bummy back in the big time I can lead the respectable life I've always longed for. I'll find out what he's got in this bag. He must carry the keys. Come, let's work out the details.

> *She and Madge go off.*

WINKLEMAN: Why didn't I retire two years ago, when I was ahead? Lead a quiet life? Write the Comedy Humane of New York? Maybe I was afraid to be left alone with my distorted heart. Oh, here comes my cousin. *Exit.*

> *Bummidge and Bertram enter. Bummidge is holding a child's potty.*

BUMMIDGE: Bert, this was a real piece of luck. This is just like the one Mama sat me on. It will help me to re-enter my infancy.

BERTRAM: You won't sit on that during the broadcast, will you?

BUMMIDGE: I'm not sure. But the Ego has hung a veil, the veil of infantile amnesia, over the earliest facts of life. I have to tear it down. See the bare truth . . .

BERTRAM: Can it be done?

BUMMIDGE: Shush! *Finger to lips*: A quiet corner. A bit of reverie. We were all *body* once. Then we split.

BERTRAM: The trauma . . .

Pamela comes in.

BUMMIDGE: O Trauma. O Regression—Sublimation! I think this is a good spot.

> *He squats behind the sofa, so that only his head is visible.*

BERTRAM, *catching sight of Pamela*: Don't get settled yet.

BUMMIDGE: The mighty of the earth have put us in this position, and it's from here we must make our stand. This is a very small pot.

> *Bertram whispers to him.*

Why didn't you say so?

BERTRAM: Get a grip on yourself.

PAMELA: Lover?

BUMMIDGE—*leaps up*: Just as I was beginning to feel something. Bert, go clear everything with Mott. There's still that headache about the money. Where's Aufschnitt with the coat? If these people trip me up before the broadcast, I'll murder them, cut my throat, and set fire to the building.

Exit Bertram.

PAMELA: What are you doing?

BUMMIDGE: Therapy, dear. Therapy. I didn't expect to see you.

PAMELA: On a day like this? I came to help.

BUMMIDGE: Help? You? That's a new one. Where have you been?

PAMELA: Thinking of you. Of your ideas. Our future. *Sits on sofa.*

BUMMIDGE, *pulling up a chair beside her*: Where were you last night? I phoned and phoned.

PAMELA: Why, darling, I was visiting Mother. You forgot.

BUMMIDGE: That madam? The hell you were.

PAMELA: We went out to U.S. One for a pizza pie. I told her how mad I am for you, and how happy we'd be if you became a professor of dramatic psychology. I'm sure Johns Hopkins will offer you the chair.

BUMMIDGE: There are times when I wish you didn't have that vapid look. I do love you, in my peculiar way.

PAMELA: A quiet, decent life. Straight. A real home.

BUMMIDGE: I've figured out the main forms of love. A man can love a woman on the tenderness system. That's very good. Or on the lust system. That's better than nothing. Or on the pride system. That's worse than nothing.

PAMELA: My lover! *Embracing him*: Your stomach is rumbling.

BUMMIDGE: It isn't rumbling. It's doing free association.

PAMELA: You're brain all over. Sheer brain.

> *They rise and move toward barber chair.*

BUMMIDGE: Sweetheart—that diamond anklet—*points*— Bought when I was flush. I paid Tiffany twelve grand.

PAMELA: Kiss me, Bummy, hold me close. *Goes through his pockets; gets the key to the valise.*

BUMMIDGE: I could pawn it for five. Louie Mott would take it.

> *They are now back to back. Bummidge holds Pamela's ankle and removes her shoe. She, meanwhile, is opening the valise.*

PAMELA: All my life I've looked for nothing but peace, security, quiet, but I always wind up in some absurd mixup.

BUMMIDGE: You have big feet.

PAMELA: You swept me off them like a force of nature.

BUMMIDGE, *removing the anklet*: I've got it! *They begin to part.*

PAMELA: It's opening. Thousands! *Turning to face him*: You've got thousands here.

BUMMIDGE: But earmarked for a higher purpose. I can't use them.

PAMELA: My anklet! Give it back!

BUMMIDGE: Where did you get the keys? Shut my valise.

PAMELA: You thief!

BUMMIDGE: Calling *me* a thief?

> *He shuts and locks the valise while Pamela tries to recover the anklet. Louie Mott runs in.*

MOTT: Your wife is below—Bella.

BUMMIDGE: Keep her away. . . . I don't want to see her.

MOTT: Can't you hear her hollering?

> *Enter Bertram.*

BERTRAM: Bummy, your estranged Missis!

BUMMIDGE, *to Pamela*: You'd better go.

PAMELA: Without my jewels? Like hell I will. *In a temper*: I came to help you.

BUMMIDGE: The screaming, the scratching, the hairpulling— you'll kill my broadcast. My scientific demonstration—the biggest thing in my life.

PAMELA: I won't go. Get rid of her. I'll wait.

BERTRAM: Where'll we put you? In the toilet? The broom closet?

PAMELA: I'd see you dead first, you creep.

MOTT: What about the fire escape?

PAMELA: I'll wait on the fire escape a few minutes. No longer. It's going to drizzle. And give me the anklet. My diamonds!

BUMMIDGE: Later, dear, later.

> *Bertram and Mott hurry Pamela to the fire escape.*

Lock that door. Lock her out. Oh, my character has created another typical crisis. What crazy things we are! The repetition compulsion. *To statue of Freud*: O, Master, how deep you were! . . . Imogen! Where is she? Astray again? That poor sexual waif. Louie, pull the shade.

> *We now see nothing of Pamela but an occasional silhouette through the shade.*

How am I going to get rid of Bella?

> *Exit with Bertram. Enter Imogen.*

IMOGEN: Did Mr. Bummidge call me?

MOTT: Imogen, as soon as I see you my pulses double and triple. Don't ask a man to waste such feelings.

IMOGEN—*fights him off*: Mr. Mott, don't. It's almost broadcast time.

MOTT: A flash! A red haze. And from below I get this gentle, gentle heat. Here. Feel . . . Where's your hand?

> *Pounding at the door, right.*

IMOGEN, *struggling*: Someone's coming.

MOTT, *all over her*: I'm oblivious!

IMOGEN: You look so . . . icky.

MOTT: It's virility. You'll be astonished. Ecstatic. Wait till you see.

> *Someone is battering the door. Mott, blowing a kiss, takes off. Imogen's stockings are falling. Her dress has been pulled off the shoulders.*

IMOGEN: How did he get to my garter belt? . . . Who is it? *Trying to fasten her stockings*: Coming . . .

> *She opens the door. Enter Aufschnitt, carrying a coat on a hanger and wrapped in brown paper.*

AUFSCHNITT, *crossing*: Is Mr. Bummidge here? I am his tailor.

IMOGEN: I thought you were his wife.

AUFSCHNITT: I came with the coat for his broadcast. But, please, I need C.O.D.

> *Enter Bella, large and aggressive, pushing past them into the room, outlandishly dressed. One can see that Pamela has made a study of Bummidge's wife in order to give him—or pretend to give him—all that Bella could never conceivably offer.*

BELLA: Where is he, that miserable man? And where is that cheap lay of his? I'll clobber them both. Then let them go on television with bloody faces.

AUFSCHNITT: Mrs. Bummidge, I have your husband's coat. But this time he must pay.

BELLA: I don't blame you. He wanted squalor, did he? Ugh! No self-respecting dog would throw up here. Imogen, tell him I've come. *Sits*.

IMOGEN: I'll try and find him. *Exit*.

BELLA: He's somewhere near, listening.

> *She looks for him. We see Pamela's silhouette. We hear the rumble of thunder. Enter Bertram, instructed to get rid of Bella.*

BERTRAM: Mrs. Bummidge, are you looking for your husband?

BELLA: So, where is the great mental wizard? Ah, it's the ratcatcher. How can he bear to have you around? You must get your suits in the morgue. They smell like it. Where is he?

BERTRAM: They're building that dam in the Nile. Abu Simbel. He wanted to have a look at those Pharaohs before the water covers them.

Enter Bummidge as a little boy, playing hopscotch.

BELLA: So. With his psychology he's gone back to childhood. Here's our kiddy. Some people fade or subside, but not him. He'll go through every agony. How old are you, little man?

BUMMIDGE: Six and a half.

BELLA, *to Bert*: I wish he had gone to Ethiopia, you stooge. *To Bummidge*: And are you a good little boy?

BUMMIDGE: Oh, yes, otherwise my parents hit me with rulers. They slash me with straps. So I am.

BELLA: And what are you going to be when you grow up?

BUMMIDGE: With wings, but on foot like a goose.

AUFSCHNITT: Mr. Bummidge, are you ready for the coat?

BUMMIDGE—*looks at coat, pleased*: Ah!

AUFSCHNITT: So pay me.

BUMMIDGE—*face changing, he examines the coat*: What kind of a garment do you call this? Is that a buttonhole? Aufschnitt, have you lost all pride in your work?

AUFSCHNITT: Pride I can't eat. Pride doesn't pay the rent.

Bummidge stands on the platform as Aufschnitt fits the coat, a garment resembling the one worn by the late Mr. Nehru.

BUMMIDGE: Affluence is finished. People are poor again. I've paid you thousands.

AUFSCHNITT: Not a cent in two years. In two years! What do I know from affluence!

BELLA, *laughing at Bummidge in his coat*: Look at that! What a freak he is! Now you'll pay what—sixty G's?—to play the psychiatrist to that howling gang at the Waldorf.

BUMMIDGE: Who's howling? Have you been there?

BELLA: Certainly, and a rummier bunch I never saw. Gobbling up the caviar and lushing champagne. Who *are* those scientists? *She puts her purse on chair near him and strides about.*

BUMMIDGE—*when her back is turned examines her purse*: You saw the gate-crashers. You have to expect some of that at every affair. Now Bella, sweetheart . . .

BELLA—*snatches away her purse, shouting*: Don't you pull that sweetheart stuff on me, after my years of misery! I'll never let you snow me again.

BUMMIDGE, *angrily, pursuing her about stage as Aufschnitt tries to fit the coat*: Then what do you want? These fights with me are your bread and meat.

BELLA: I've come. I have my reasons, never mind. Legally I'm still your wife.

BUMMIDGE: You took everything. Two million dollars' worth

of property. I have to squabble with ingrate buttonhole makers.

AUFSCHNITT, *running after him*: Don't move your arms too much. It's a rush job. The seams are weak.

BELLA: I had to stop you from squandering every last cent on broads. Especially this last one—the choreographer. A fancy word for whore.

BUMMIDGE, *again on the platform*: Don't talk like that. She loves me.

BELLA: Love? Don't talk to me about love. I've seen the bills.

> *The Technician enters with a kit and begins to apply make-up to Bummidge's face.*

TECHNICIAN: Let's see you under the lights. Your skin is peculiar.

BELLA: You took her to Europe on that disastrous tour of old opera houses. Me you left behind. You think Pamela loves you for your personality? For your brilliant mind? For your bad bridgework? And your belching, and getting up ten times a night to pee, so a person can't sleep? Is that what she loves you for? *Her eye is caught by an open newspaper.* Oh, General Electric, down three-eighths.

BUMMIDGE, *smoothing the front of his coat*: Bella, you're distracting me from my great purpose. Keep the two millions, but stop bothering me.

TECHNICIAN: Let me see what I can do with this complexion of yours.

> *He drags a complaining Bummidge to the barber chair.*

BELLA: You sent me on phony errands to clear the decks for your orgies. I was a prisoner for six months on that milk farm in Wisconsin.

BUMMIDGE: Overweight. We had to think of your blood pressure.

BELLA: You put a pistol in my night table to suggest suicide.

BUMMIDGE: Maybe I wanted you to shoot me. *To Technician*: I want you to emphasize the serenity of my brow and my eyes. Let's eliminate this clownish slant.

BELLA—*as she comes over to the barber chair we hear a rumble of thunder*: Bummy, tell me the truth. What's going to happen? I can't understand. I'm just an old-fashioned, goodhearted broad, an ordinary, practical, loyal woman.

BUMMIDGE, *to Technician*: Recognize the party line?

> *The Technician makes a broad grimace of agreement, but continues working.*

BELLA: At one time, to me, you were everything. Why don't you explain it to me? . . . I think we're going to have a thundershower.

BUMMIDGE, *with an anxious glance toward the fire escape*: Listen, Bella, in eighteen fifty-nine Darwin published *The Origin of Species*; nineteen hundred, Freud came out with *The Interpretation of Dreams*.

BELLA: For God's sake, Bummy, have a little pride. Don't go tell those intellectuals what they already know. Elementary. They'll laugh at you.

BUMMIDGE: They know *nothing* about laughing. That's my field. . . . Bella, there's something I can't forgive you. Never. *Leaves the chair.*

BELLA—*Follows him*: What, now? What?

BUMMIDGE: You want to be a business power, a tycoon. Well, you took the old building where I played in youth, the Trilby Theatre, and rented it for a meat market. Where names like "Bummidge," like "Jimmy Savo," used to be on the marquee, we now have "The Kalbfuss Palace of Meats. Pork Butts Today."

BELLA, *giving no ground*: So what?

BUMMIDGE: I'm going to restore it, rededicate it to comedy.

BELLA: Bring back vaudeville?

BUMMIDGE: No. I want to open it to the public. I want to make it a theatre of the soul. Let people come off the street to practice my *Existenz*-Action-Self-analysis. Tickets at modest prices. Let the public step up and work with me—my method.

BELLA: You want to bring psychoanalysis to the vaudeville stage?

BUMMIDGE: You can't get the whole public on the couch. Theories have to be socially active, broad. The couch is for higher-income brackets. Bella, people make a career of their problems, a racket of their characters, an occupation of their personality traits. Take yourself, for instance. *Parodies her*: "An old-fashioned, goodhearted broad. To me you were everything." . . . How you belt it out! The throbbing heart! And love! Jesus, what a production you make of love! Warfare, that's what you really love. You spend your whole life playing the dramatic values of your Devotion, your Fate, your Sacrifice and Struggles. What corn! Aren't you ashamed of yourself? Bella, only laughter can save you from this. Such elaboration of personality is a joke.

BELLA, *stunned by this*: Reopen the Trilby. That's Utopian. Crazy. . . . Oh, one man's jokes are another man's theories. I don't get it.

BUMMIDGE: In this valise I have almost enough to buy the lease from Kalbfuss. Oh, Lord, and I have to scrape up the balance for Louie. *Runs to desk*. Somewhere in this mess is the receipt from Tiffany's. *Pulls out drawers*. Ah, here. More than I thought. Fourteen thousand.

AUFSCHNITT: I don't dare leave this coat without you pay me. My wife warned me.

BUMMIDGE: Bella, maybe you've got a few bucks.

BELLA: A headache from your theories, that's what I've got.

> *Enter Bertram.*

Do you have aspirins in the medicine chest? I'm sure you have rats in that bathroom. Where's the light? *Exit*.

BERTRAM: I'll show you. . . . Rats?

AUFSCHNITT: Mr. Bummidge, you say plain, ordinary people could understand your psychology? I have plenty of trouble in my family. A sad daughter who won't even get out of bed.

BUMMIDGE: Single?

AUFSCHNITT: The bed or the daughter? . . . Both single.

> *Enter Imogen.*

BUMMIDGE: Perhaps you and I could work together. Free of charge, of course.

AUFSCHNITT: For nothing?

IMOGEN: Mr. Bummidge, you have very little time.

BUMMIDGE: For instance.

IMOGEN: He's never too busy to hold out a hand to misery.

BUMMIDGE: Now Aufschnitt, listen to me.

IMOGEN: It's started to rain.

BUMMIDGE: Bertram, find an umbrella for you-know-who. Aufschnitt, I am six years old. My parents have bought me my first pair of galoshes for school. Gleaming black rubber, and such a delicious smell. They make beautiful tracks in the snow. But my mother warns me—the usual: We are poor people. You lose everything. Don't you come home without those galoshes. Papa will kill you stone dead!

> *Bertram frantically looks for an umbrella. Pamela tries to make herself heard through the glass door. Bertram can find nothing but a little girl's pink parasol. When he opens the door a crack, Pamela tries to fight her way in. He succeeds in locking the door.*

BERTRAM: It's raining out there. A regular monsoon.

BUMMIDGE: Listen, Aufschnitt, my first-grade teacher, Miss Farnum, was a youthful rhubarb blonde. You be Miss Farnum, and I'll be six.

AUFSCHNITT: What should I do?

BUMMIDGE: Act and feel like my teacher.

> *Enter Max and a private detective, Mr. Galluppo.*

MAX: Pop, Mr. Galluppo, here, is my lawyer, a private investigator.

BUMMIDGE: He looks like a blackmailer. I have no time for this.

MAX: Listen to his report.

GALLUPPO, *gazing about*: So this is what happens to stars in retirement. Substandard housing.

AUFSCHNITT: I'm not sure I can imitate a young teacher in a long dress.

BUMMIDGE: Of course you can. Do it for your daughter. This can help her. Like this. *Enacts Miss Farnum.*

AUFSCHNITT: Like this? *He tries.*

BUMMIDGE: Quite good for a first effort.

AUFSCHNITT: How could it help my poor daughter Joy?

BUMMIDGE: Concentrate with me, Aufschnitt. The other kids with their sheepskins and boots have gone home. But where are my galoshes?

> *He and Aufschnitt hunt under chairs for the galoshes.*

MAX, *to Galluppo*: Give your report on his friend Pamela. Where was she last night?

GALLUPPO: In premises at Six-Y Jones Street. She had relations with a gentleman of the other sex. Every night a different person.

BUMMIDGE, *with some hauteur*: You must have the wrong party. Miss Sillerby is an artist from a distinguished Southern family. *To Aufschnitt*: Now, Miss Farnum, I'm in a terrible spot. First you scold me. Then you make fun of me. You stick out your tongue. I start to bawl. . . . Max, why do you do this?

AUFSCHNITT: Now little boy, you'd better not cry.

> *Enter Mott. The Technician appears above.*

MOTT: We've got to have a sound level, Bummy. Swing out the boom, John.

GALLUPPO: Is this a photo of the party in question?

MAX: You bet. Show it to my father.

IMOGEN, *trying to interpose herself*: Oh, don't do that. You'll upset everything.

BUMMIDGE: That's what he wants to do.

> *Galluppo shows photo to Aufschnitt, who can't bear to look.*

AUFSCHNITT: Why me? I don't recognize these people. They have no clothes on.

GALLUPPO: Monday with a Wall Street broker. Tuesday with a bartender. Wednesday the super of her building.

BUMMIDGE: I'm crying over my galoshes. I'm not a day over six.

AUFSCHNITT: What a little crybaby! *Puts out his tongue.*

BUMMIDGE: She tried to make me laugh at my dread. I hated her for it. But she was right. She tried to teach me to reject ridiculous pain. *He pounds at door of the fire escape, where we see Pamela's anguished figure in silhouette.*

TECHNICIAN: What's he doing? What goes on?

IMOGEN: It's a cloudburst. They always affect him.

MOTT: Let's try those lights. Bert, give a hand here. Bummy, you've got only twenty minutes.

BUMMIDGE: What? *Shakes his fist at door, then turns from it.* Louie, take these rocks. Tiffany's. Here's the receipt. Worth eight grand at least. Oh Bummidge, you sucker, you patsy, you mark! Max, take this snooper away. It's nearly time for my broadcast. Louie, let's go.

AUFSCHNITT: Crybaby! Crybaby!

BUMMIDGE: I should have laughed, not wept. *Tries laughter.*

MAX: There'll be no broadcast.

> *Enter Bella.*

Mother, what are you doing here?

BELLA, *pointing to Galluppo*: Where did he come from? Does he do work for you too? I pay him fat fees. He takes from us both for the same information, I bet.

GALLUPPO: I didn't know you was related.

AUFSCHNITT: Crybaby! Crybaby!

BELLA: Shut up! My head is splitting.

> *Enter Winkleman and Madge.*

I knew they'd show up!

TECHNICIAN, *holding up microphone*: Let's hear you speak a word or two.

BUMMIDGE: Help! Help!

> *Galluppo forces him to look at the photo.*

Oh, the bitch!

> *There is a sharp rapping at the door. Lights are tested. Cables are draped over furniture. Enter a messenger.*

What do you want?

MESSENGER: Western Union.

IMOGEN: I'll take the wire.

> *Enter Aunt Velma in a wheelchair. She carries a cane.*

WINKLEMAN: Here's Mother.

BUMMIDGE: Tante Velma! She's come!

VELMA: Why is it so crowded and noisy?

BUMMIDGE: You were midwife at my birth. From the sightless universe into your hands!

> *Telephone rings.*

Bertram, answer.

BERTRAM: Shouldn't I open that door?

BELLA: Is that a woman screaming somewhere?

BUMMIDGE: The wind! Wind and rain!

MADGE, *persuasive, cooperative*: Now listen to me, Bummy.

BUMMIDGE, *mistaking her tone*: You and Winkie are plotting against me. A conspiracy.

MADGE: But that's just paranoid.

AUFSCHNITT: You must pay me or I can't let you have the coat. *Tries to remove it.*

BUMMIDGE: Bella, won't you get this needle-pusher off my back?

BELLA: How much?

AUFSCHNITT: One twenty-five.

MAX—*tries to stop her*: Mother, don't.

BELLA, *fishing money out of her bosom*: You've ruined my life, but thank God I'm comfortably ruined.

BERTRAM: It's Doctor Ratzenhofer on the phone. He says how long will the broadcast be? He has appointments.

BUMMIDGE: Oh, Doctor Ratzenhofer?

WINKLEMAN: How can you start in all this chaos?

MOTT: How do I know these diamonds aren't paste?

IMOGEN: The wire is from Kalbfuss. He's standing by.

BUMMIDGE: Kalbfuss! *Throws his arms upward*. Thank heaven for his loyalty.

AUFSCHNITT: The seams! The seams are opening!

BELLA: These are the fruits of my husband's originality. Confusion!

VELMA, *rapping with her cane*: I think this floor is sagging.

BUMMIDGE: A mere symbol, Tante.

WINKLEMAN: Look here, Cousin, you've got Madge and me all wrong.

BELLA, *pushing forward*: We know about you. Starving old people. Conditions worse than Andersonville. Investigations. The whole story about to break. A hell of a note.

BUMMIDGE: You've all come to prevent my broadcast.

MAX: That's right.

GALLUPPO, *pulling out a paper*: I have a restraining order.

BELLA, *to Max*: Don't try to shaft your father. He's got it coming from me.

BUMMIDGE: You want to make a farce of my serious intentions. But someone has to do something. Even if that someone is only me.

> *Mott is about to hit the diamonds with a hammer to see if they are real.*

Hold it!

> *Bummidge restrains Mott. There is silence. Then Bummidge laughs strangely.*

Ladies and gentlemen, I invite you to witness a typical moment of human existence, showing mankind as it makes the most of its universal opportunities, amid all the miracles of light and motion. . . .

> *The next group of speeches is spoken together, jumbled.*

MAX: Now he's Cassandra.

MADGE: I never know what he's talking about. Let's start.

VELMA: Why did I even come? Family feeling? Big deal!

GALLUPPO: Fifty bucks an hour, I charge.

WINKLEMAN: We can't let this go on!

> *They fall silent.*

BUMMIDGE, *violently*: Stop! Why are you here? I am your food, your prey. You have filled my life with stench and noise; dogged me night and day; lived on me like green fungus on pumpernickel. But you won't be happy till I'm crucified? You, a Roman crowd? I, an Asiatic slave?

MAX: Man, now he's on the Jesus kick.

BUMMIDGE—*holds up both hands, fingers widely spread*: Shall I submit?

WINKLEMAN, *trying vainly to soothe him*: Please come off it, Bummy. Don't be carried away.

MADGE: You'll forget your purpose.

VELMA: This is New York. Nineteen sixty-five A.D.

BUMMIDGE: All right, where is that staple gun? Imogen. *He stands on the desk. Imogen approaches with the stapler.* Staple Bummidge to the wall.

> *Imogen hesitates. Bertram staples Bummidge's cuffs. His arms are outstretched.*

MAX: The martyrdom bit!

WINKLEMAN: Wasted! He's using up his energy before the broadcast. Wait, Bummy.

MADGE: Save it for the cameras.

TECHNICIAN: I'm impressed.

GALLUPPO: Maybe I am a lousy crook, a double-dealing fink, but this is blasphemy.

IMOGEN: Not with Mr. Bummidge. It's real! Can't you see he's in pain? He's having an attack of Humanitis. Catch him.

BELLA: No, Bummy, no! I take it all back.

> *Pamela, drenched, with the parasol, has forced her way in. She is gasping.*

MOTT: We got just a little time before the broadcast. *To Technician*: Let's take a five-minute break.

They kneel and shoot dice.

BELLA, *as Pamela collapses at Bummidge's feet*: There's the whore in the picture. Now we got the full cast.

MOTT: Okay. Roll 'em.

BUMMIDGE: Forgive them, Father, for, for . . . What comes next?

CURTAIN

ACT TWO

Minutes later: Bummidge has been extricated from his coat, which hangs empty on the wall. Onstage are Pamela, who has wrapped herself, shivering, in the tapestry on the barber chair; Aufschnitt, who is taking down the coat in order to mend it; Madge, explaining the situation to Max and Galluppo. Bella appears skeptical but is really (as always) passionately in pursuit of her life's project: involvement with her husband's magical peculiarities. Tante Velma, legs boldly crossed, sits in her wheelchair smoking a cigar and studying business documents. Her kindly old eyeglasses have been pushed up on her forehead; without them she looks tough and severe. Mott is looking at his wristwatch.

MOTT: We may have to call it all off.

MADGE: Nonsense! Too much is riding on Bummy for us all. Max understands now.

MAX: I see what you mean. I get it. He's going to do this anyway. We can't overcome his peculiar ideas, so we exploit them instead. Smart.

BELLA: You *think* you can outsmart him. Wait. You'll see how shifty and shrewd he is.

MADGE: Winkie is in the library with him, explaining that we offer full cooperation. All of us.

GALLUPPO: But what will CBS, NBC, MCA, Fiddleman, and the rest see in his shenanigans?

MAX: Madge and Winkie are right. There's nothing so extreme or kookie that the mass media won't try to use it. We talk of atomic explosion and population explosion, but in the twentieth century there's also an explosion of consciousness. Society needs the imagination of its most alienated members. They want to defy it? It doesn't care. It pays them millions. Money reconciles all tendencies.

VELMA: You're your father's son. You sound like him.

PAMELA: I'm soaked to the skin.

BELLA, *acid*: Undress. By now everybody knows how you look in the nude.

PAMELA: Without your corsets, you must be like a sea cow.

BELLA: The government should label people the way it does meat—prime, choice, and dog food.

PAMELA: You have a plain label—the ball-breaking wife.

> *Bella is about to strike Pamela with her purse; Pamela prepares to defend herself with her high-heeled shoe; Max restrains his mother.*

MOTT: Minutes ticking away!

VELMA, *to Aufschnitt as he passes with the coat*: And what's he doing?

AUFSCHNITT: Mending the raiment. *Exit.*

MAX: The thing is, what will I get out of it?

MADGE: You? You're the heir.

VELMA: With Papa in the big money again? And doting on his sonny boy? Ha, *ha!*

PAMELA: So far, I've lost my anklet.

Mott covertly lifts it from his pocket and looks at it.

MADGE, *suspicious*: Louie . . .

Enter Imogen and Bertram. Bertram carries an infant in his arms.

BERTRAM: Bummy wanted to see a little child. Where is he?

Enter Bummidge with Winkleman.

IMOGEN: Mr. Bummidge—an infant!

BUMMIDGE, *excited*: Undress it. I must see the original human material. The essential thing.

BELLA, *taking charge*: This child could use a clean diaper.

BERTRAM: Her mother is an alcoholic. I had to give her a twenty-dollar deposit.

IMOGEN: In the bar, across the street.

BUMMIDGE, *enraptured*: Look at this freedom! How the little belly rises and falls. The state of Nature! Life drifts into the infant. . . . *Laves himself with air*. Drifts, drifts. Precious, blessed infancy. Everything loathsome about the human species is forgiven time after time, and with every child we begin again.

GALLUPPO: I don't dig it.

IMOGEN, *explaining*: Heaven lies about us in our infancy. Then comes repression. We lose Eternity. We get shut up in Time.

VELMA—*gestures with her cigar, looks upward*: Big deal. I delivered thousands of them, poor things.

MOTT: Bummy, it's practically zero hour.

Aufschnitt enters with the coat.

BUMMIDGE: Take the baby, Bertram. Wait, I must have one last look. *He looks tenderly at infant, as if to memorize it.*

AUFSCHNITT: I fixed the seams.

BERTRAM: I'm out of pocket twenty bucks.

BUMMIDGE—*as he is getting into the coat, looks at Bella*: Bella . . .

BELLA: On twenty bucks the mother'll go on a two-day binge. Oh, well . . . *digs again into her bosom.*

> *Bertram takes money and goes, with the infant under one arm.*

PAMELA—*comes forward*: Bummy, I have to have dry clothes. And where's my anklet?

BUMMIDGE—*hurries to large wicker clothes hamper, opens it*: Here's something for you. *Struck by an idea*: There's something here for each of you. . . . Ah, yes. For each and every one. Marvelous! You'll all participate with me in the broadcast. Louie, throw away the old format.

WINKLEMAN: Ad lib? Now? But Bummy—think!

BUMMIDGE: I've never been so lucid. That little infant shows me the way. All impulse. Impulse is the soul of freedom. My deeper self is telling me what to do. *Clutches his head, but smilingly.*

PAMELA, *unfolding the garment*: Why, this is nothing but a burlesque stripper's outfit!

BUMMIDGE, *to Winkleman*: You said everyone would stand behind me.

MADGE: To a man! I remember Doctor Ehrlich and the magic bullet.

WINKLEMAN: And Semmelweiss, and Pasteur!

MOTT: Don't forget Richard Nixon. How against him they all were until he went on television with that little dog.

BUMMIDGE: And Pamela? You, too?

PAMELA, *somewhat reluctant*: Yes, Bummy. You'll give back my diamonds, won't you? *Exit.*

BUMMIDGE, *as he watches her go*: The forms—the many forms that suffering takes. The compulsion to suffer. But for each and every one of these there is a method to evade suffering. Delusion. Intoxication. Ecstasy. And comedy. I must remember that for the broadcast. Now listen, all of you. I'm going back to my sources and you'll all wear costumes and step forward as I call on you. Imogen, hand them out. Louie, the hoodlum you were during Prohibition.

> *Mott goes to change.*

Madge, this flapper's dress with fringes.

> *Madge goes.*

Max, you'll represent my father. You resemble him.

> *Max puts on a shopkeeper's apron and a broad-brimmed hat.*

Bella, a bridal gown.

> *Bella goes.*

Winkie. These rompers.

WINKLEMAN: Must I?

BUMMIDGE: Your cooperation is essential.

> *Winkleman goes.*

There's a reason why they're all so obliging. Woe unto you when all men shall speak well of you.

> *Enter Bertram.*

But it's woe anyway, wherever you look. Imogen, dear, will you assist?

IMOGEN: Of course, Mr. Bummidge.

VELMA: Where do I come in?

BUMMIDGE: Give the old bat this hat with fruit. Bertram, in my unconscious it turns out you have female characteristics. Wear this dress.

BERTRAM, *accepting*: Female? Curious!

BUMMIDGE: Isn't it? *He marvels briefly.*

IMOGEN: Mr. Bummidge, are you sure you know what you're doing?

BUMMIDGE: It is the right thing, my child—whatever *that* is. I feel inward confidence. Aufschnitt . . .

AUFSCHNITT: Am I in the broadcast too? I've never been on television.

BUMMIDGE: Man! That's who you'll be. Repressed, civilized Man. Poor humankind in bondage. Thread in your fingers and chains on your feet.

GALLUPPO: And me?

BUMMIDGE: Sly, smiling, menacing . . . I have it! Bella's father. Grinning, then violent. Yes!

Enter Technician.

TECHNICIAN: Where's the opening setup?

Enter Mott dressed as a neighborhood tough.

MOTT: Places! Let's have lights.

BUMMIDGE: Louie, iris in on me here, by this statue of Freud.

IMOGEN: I'm dying of excitement!

MOTT: Time! Five, four, three, two, one—you're on.

BUMMIDGE—*begins an attempt at smiling refinement*: Ladies and gentlemen of the psychiatric world. Honored guests. You know me, of course, as a comedian. But today I invite you to put away that old image. Look at this person, one of yourselves, a human being. See this hair, these eyes, these wattles, stubby hands, a heart that beats: Philip Bummidge, sixty years old. Sixty-one years ago I was literally nothing. I was merely possible. Then I was conceived, and became inevitable. When I die, I shall be *im*possible. Meanwhile, between two voids, past and future, I exist. Medically, I seem quite sound, though not in my first youth. Strong as a horse. *Feels his muscles.* Twenty-twenty vision. *Pulls down his underlids.* Powerful lungs. *Shouts*: Hoy! *Pauses.* Nothing wrong with the organism, hey? But up here. *Suddenly gloomy*: My mind! Inside my skull. My feelings, my emotions. *Quite tragically*: My personality, my mind! My mind has a will of its own. This psyche of mine is an outlaw. Can this be the normal human state? Is this what we are meant to be? Oh, my character! How did I ever get stuck with these monstrous peculiarities? Why so vivid within, so dead outside? I feel like a museum of all the perversity, sickness, and ugliness of mankind. Oh, Death, take me or leave me, but don't haunt me any more. But you see, ladies and gentlemen, brothers and sisters, it's because of death that we are individuals. Organisms without death have no true identity. But we are what we are owing to our morbidity. *In earnest*: I bless the day when I discovered how abnormal I was. I read all the books and, never forgetting that I was an actor, a comedian, I formed my own method. I learned to obtain self-knowledge by doing what I best knew how to do, acting out the main events of my life, dragging repressed material into the open by sheer force of drama. I'm not solely a man but also a man who is an artist, and an artist whose sphere is comedy. Though the conditions may be impossible, laughter in decay, there is nothing else for me to do but face those real conditions. *The lecturer*: A general increase of consciousness in civilized people accompanied by a decrease in the value they attach to themselves and one another is a prime condition. *Dissatisfied with his own pomposity*: But rather than lecture, I prefer to illustrate. Let me introduce, briefly, certain friends and relatives.

> *In the following scene, people come forward as called, in their costumes.*

This is Aunt Velma, who delivered me. This, my tender bride. This is my son, who will represent my father. This proper lady is my sister. This is my colleague, Bertram, a mother figure.

> *Enter Winkleman in a Lord Fauntleroy costume.*

Oh, yes, this is my cousin Winkie, whose mother always dressed him absurdly.

WINKLEMAN: Excuse these knickers—one must humor a client, a man of genius with brilliant ideas.

Enter Pamela, wearing her strip-tease costume.

BUMMIDGE: This little lady has offered to represent the grandeur and misery of the erotic life. She's something of an expert on this subject. These unfortunates are part of me, and I of them. Now, my method, on the most elementary level, opens a channel to the past. Like that old song—*sings*—"I'm just a kid again, doin' what I did again."

All sing in chorus. He leads them forward. The group stands about him.

I am convinced that lies are bad art. I reclaim my freedom by acting. I tear down the Bastille of censorship and distortion. No more isolation. Break out of jail! We must leap beyond repression. But look at these miserable creatures. I shall start with one of them, my old aunt. *Wheels her forward*. Tante, you bridge many generations, and you have a long memory.

VELMA: Like an old filing case, I am.

BUMMIDGE: Was mine a difficult birth?

VELMA: On your father's scales you weighed fourteen pounds. You gave lots of pain. It was tough, but I pulled you through.

BUMMIDGE, *to camera*: She thinks she's being funny. *To her*:—Now, when was I weaned?

VELMA: Late. On the way to Prospect Park, on your mama's lap, your feet were dragging on the floor of the streetcar. You didn't want the breast and your mama said, "All right, I'll give it to the conductor."

BUMMIDGE, *to camera*: An old gag. She's full of them. They're really sadistic threats in comic form.—Now, when was I toilet-trained?

VELMA: My sister and I kept clean houses. As soon as you could sit up.

BUMMIDGE, *somberly*: This is very bad!

MADGE: Was it so serious?

BUMMIDGE: Ah, Madge—my sister, my poor companion in abuse. Terrible! They ruined us. This is horrible information.

BELLA: Don't take it so hard.

BUMMIDGE: I never had a chance. How can I hold my head up?

VELMA: But nobody could keep you clean. You made in your pants. You were a wild, disobedient boy, like your Uncle Mitchell.

BUMMIDGE: Yes, tell everyone about him. *To television audience*: She thinks she's irresistible.

VELMA: He played baseball. Shortstop. The bus with his team fell in the Passaic River. It damaged his brains. On the Sea Beach Express, he exposed himself to some girls from the shirtwaist factory.

BUMMIDGE, *to camera*: This is her lifelong patter. Old lobster shells of wit. The meat is gone.—Tell the people more. . . .

VELMA: Then there was Uncle Harold. He was a saxophone performer. On the Weehawken Ferry. During the War, he passed the hat for the boys Over There.

MAX: But he put the money in his own pocket.

VELMA: He needed a start in business. That branch of the family did all right. Furthermore . . .

BUMMIDGE: Enough. She comes on like a charming old thing. From her jokes, you'd never guess what viciousness there was in her.

> *Velma spreads her mouth with her fingers and makes a horrid face at him.*

WINKLEMAN, *sternly*: Mother! On the air!

VELMA: Should I say more? Should I tell about Aunt Rose? *Parodying her own family sentiments*: All Perth Amboy listened in the street when she sang. Such a woice!

BUMMIDGE: No, enough. Take her away, Winkie.

VELMA: Give me a light, my child. *Cigar, again.*

BUMMIDGE: Infinite sadness salted with jokes. But . . . *Lecturing*: My method—as follows: I have trained myself to re-enter any phase of my life, at will. By bouncing a ball, rolling a hoop, sucking my thumb, I become a child. When I want to visit the remote parts of my mind, I take to the couch. *Lies down.* Doctor, I had a dream. *As analyst*: Tell me all about it. *As patient*: I dreamt I was at sea in an old shoebox. *Rising*: Thus, ladies and gentlemen, I was able to isolate a hard core of problems, by adapting the methods of Freud—that Genius! *Turns emotionally to bust*: The disease I discovered in myself, I call Humanitis. An emotional disorder of our relation to the human condition. Suddenly, being human is too much for me. I faint, and stagger. *He enacts the sick man. Holds dialogue with himself*: "What's the matter, Bummidge? Don't you like other human beings?" "Like them! I adore them! Only I can't bear them." "I love 'em like a dog. So ardent, so smoochy. Wagging my tail.

This sick, corrupt emotion leaks out of me." I don't have the strength to bear my feelings. *Lecturing*: This is the weakness of my comedy. When the laughing stops, there's still a big surplus of pain.

BERTRAM: He's going to explain about the Pagliacci gangrene.

BUMMIDGE: The Pagliacci gangrene! Caused as all gangrene is by a failure of circulation. Cut off by self-pity. Passivity. Fear. Masochistic rage. Now—*smiling and bowing*—I shall ask you to follow me into the library, where I have prepared an exhibit of charts and diagrams.

> *Exit, followed by the Technician with camera and by Mott.*

GALLUPPO: You think you sell this? I'd walk out. Worst show I ever saw.

MAX: It's like a lecture at the New School, but crazier.

IMOGEN: Every word of it is clear to me.

BERTRAM: Plain as day.

WINKLEMAN: Take it from me, the industry is hard up for novelty. There is something here for the great public. *Desperate*: It's got to work.

MAX: If it doesn't, I've lost out on one of the biggest deals that ever came my way. My mother turned it down.

BELLA: Damn right I did.

PAMELA: I want my jewels back, at least. In this getup I deserve some consideration.

BELLA: It's a miracle you can keep them on those skinny wrists and ankles.

PAMELA: Better to be petite than built like a lady wrestler.

BELLA: Petite! Dry bones. You could do a fan dance with fly swatters.

> They begin to fight.

GALLUPPO: Here, break it up. *Takes a police grip on Pamela.*

MADGE: A cat fight is all we need. For heaven's sake, you've got to keep in line. If this fails, Winkie and I stand to lose a fortune.

BERTRAM: Bummy won't fail.

WINKLEMAN—*sweating, he tries to persuade them*: Freud has filtered down to the broad masses. He used to belong to the intellectuals and the upper middle class, but now the proles demand their share of this. As the standard of living rises, people claim the privilege of sickness, formerly one of the aristocratic prerogatives.

VELMA: Listen to my son! I had only one, but with the brains of five.

WINKLEMAN: Look! There's all this machinery of entertainment, publicity. A billion-dollar industry with administration, bureaucracy. It needs fresh material every week. And out there are millions of Americans, asking for nourishment. Bread. The industry gives 'em every substitute it can invent. Faith. I ask you to have a little faith. Haven't I always marketed whatever Bummy dreamed up?

IMOGEN: Mr. Bummidge isn't interested in being marketed.

MADGE: Isn't he? We'll see about that.

VELMA: Wheel me back. Here he comes.

> *Technician, led by Mott, comes in with camera.*

MOTT: One side. Clear it. Get Bummidge as he enters the doorway. Go, camera.

BUMMIDGE: Such, my friends, is the Pagliacci gangrene, crying as you laugh, but making a fortune meanwhile. Now let us have a brief look at my career. At twenty I sing and dance at the Old Trilby. *Sings and shuffles*:

"Oh I went to school with Maggie Moiphy
And Maggie Moiphy went to school with me-e-e.
I tried to get the best of Maggie Moiphy,
But the sonofagun, she got the best of me."

Another routine:

"Lady, lady, put out your can
I think I hear the garbage man."

As lady, answering:

"But Mister, I don't want any garbage."

Lecturing again:

By 1927 we're at the top of our fields, Coolidge and me. I tap-dance in the White House portico. *Hoofing.*

BELLA: I almost burst with pride.

BUMMIDGE, *strutting*: Three agents, two bodyguards, a fleet of Dusenbergs. Five paternity suits in one year. My own cigar vault at Dunhill's next to the Prince of Wales. I charter the Twentieth Century to take me to Saratoga for the races. People laugh at everything I say. "Nice day." *To group*: Laugh!

They laugh uproariously.

You see how it worked. "Nice day."

They laugh again. He sneezes.

AUFSCHNITT: *Gesundheit.*

BUMMIDGE: Now a dark subject. I should like to re-enact the circumstances of my marriage. I shall represent myself. Bella—Bella . . .

BELLA, *pushed forward*: Yes.

BUMMIDGE: You be Bella. The other characters will emerge as they are needed. Now, Bella, what were the first words that kicked us off into matrimony?

BELLA: The first words? It was on the telephone. I need a telephone.

> *Imogen, stooping, out of the way of camera, brings two phones. They ring. Bummidge and Bella, back to back, converse.*

BUMMIDGE: Yes? Hello?

BELLA, *breathless*: Philip?

BUMMIDGE: Yes?

BELLA: I have bad news. I'm six weeks late.

BUMMIDGE: What? What was that?

BELLA: Late! You know what I'm talking about. Do I have to draw a picture?

BUMMIDGE, *to camera*: I wouldn't have understood the picture, either. *To telephone*: From that? We were just fooling. We didn't even undress.

BELLA: I admit there wasn't much to it.

MAX: They won't spare me a single detail!

BUMMIDGE: I'll come right over. *Hangs up and speaks to camera*: Passion on a grand scale is always safe. It's that miserable, neurotic poking around that causes trouble.

PAMELA: How can he be sure she didn't do it on purpose?

BUMMIDGE: The time is now a beautiful afternoon in May. The Trifflers are having a little party in the garden.

GALLUPPO: We Trifflers are rising in the world.

MADGE: Rising into the upper lower middle class of Brooklyn.

VELMA: Lovely house. Mission-style apricot stucco.

BUMMIDGE: I am sniffing lilacs, unaware that Bella has told her parents she's knocked up. Suddenly old Triffler swoops down and says, "What did you do to my child?"

GALLUPPO, *as old Triffler*: What did you do to my child!

BUMMIDGE, *coaching*: "This you do to a father?"

GALLUPPO: This you do to a father?

BELLA: I stood under the weeping willow, when my mother ran up. *Tapping Bertram*: She hissed, "Arnold, a houseful of guests! Not now!"

BERTRAM: Arnold, a houseful of guests. Not now.

MADGE: My opinion was that they were framing him. Bella was an aggressive girl.

BELLA, *hotly*: A lot you know! But I recall the moment. My mother shouted—

VELMA: I was there. Your mother shouted, "He's so coarse! Couldn't it be a nice refined boy, you tramp? His habits are filthy. He cleans his ears in public and looks at the wax."

BELLA: She didn't call me tramp!

BUMMIDGE: She did. And she said, "Look how bad his skin is. He must have syphilis."

BELLA: She warned me you'd be a selfish husband. A hypochondriac. A tyrant. And you were. I told Mama, "He's everything you say."

MADGE: But you weren't getting any younger.

BELLA, *fiercely*: I was just a kid. My heart told me to marry him.

MADGE: Her heart! She was out to here, already. *Indicates a swollen belly.*

BUMMIDGE: Bella, you love melodrama, and you're happy when the materials of your personality turn into soap opera. You do have a sense of humor, of a grim sort, but you've neglected it.

BELLA: This proves my suffering never touched your heart. You didn't care.

BUMMIDGE: I said to Mama Triffler, "Don't you think I'm too immature to marry? I'm not ready yet."

BELLA: And you started to blubber.

BUMMIDGE: And then you hit me.

BELLA: I said, "Coward! I'll give you something to cry about!" *She strikes him.*

BUMMIDGE—*reels*: Ow! *Angry*: This was harder than the first time. *Holding his cheek*: This is very rich material.

BELLA: You tried to escape out the gate. "You people are railroading me." We were a respectable family, till we met you. You twisted our behavior into comedy.

MAX: That sounds like the truth.

BUMMIDGE: Your so-called respectability was comical without twisting. Your father tried to throttle me, is that respectable? *To Galluppo*: Choke me.

GALLUPPO: Wait a minute. What's my responsibility if there's an injury? There's a legal point, here.

BUMMIDGE, *commanding*: My method requires reliving. Choke me.

BELLA: You were just slapped.

> *A Messenger has just entered the scene.*

BUMMIDGE, *frantic*: I must have closure. We're on the air. You have to obey me.

GALLUPPO: No!

BUMMIDGE: Somebody— *To Messenger*: *You* choke me.

MADGE, *pushing the Messenger forward*: Choke him, and get it over with.

BELLA: Bummy, with all those intellectuals watching, don't be a goddamn jerk!

BUMMIDGE, *on his toes, rigid*: Choke me!

MESSENGER, *to Velma*: Hold this!

> *He brutally chokes Bummidge, who falls to his knees. Bella, Bertram, and Mott try to drag him away from his victim.*

WINKLEMAN: His face is getting purple.

IMOGEN: Enough! Stop!

MOTT—*he and Bert with difficulty pry the Messenger's fingers loose*: This fellow's a killer.

BERTRAM: Who taught you to take life like that?

MESSENGER: He asked for it. I have to grab all opportunities.

MAX: Pop, are you all right?

BUMMIDGE, *feebly*: Tip the boy. . . .

IMOGEN: It's a telegram from Mr. Fiddleman.

MADGE, *grabbing wire*: For Winkleman.

MESSENGER: What's this, a TV show? Is that Bummy? The comic?

WINKLEMAN, *reading*: Great interest, so far.

MADGE: Oh, Winkie!

Mott and Bertram throw the Messenger out.

BUMMIDGE, *to cameras*: This choking was an orgastic experience, almost. Suffering and agony can be repressive forms of gratification. Under conditions of general repression, that is how it works out. Under these conditions, man conceives the project of changing the external world, and the project of changing himself. There is no other creature that aims to change itself, or discover another kind of life. From top to bottom, each man rejects himself, denies what he is, and doesn't even know it. *He laughs. He pushes the others and forces them to laugh with him.* Isn't that funny? *General laughter.* You, too, Bert.

BERTRAM—*tries to laugh*: Heh, heh!

BUMMIDGE: Bertram is far too sick to laugh. . . . But now,

my father has learned of my transgression with Bella, and waits for me on the stoop.

MAX, *as Father*: Outcast! Now you'll marry? On what?

BUMMIDGE: His favorite punishment was to strike me under the nose with his forefinger. Exceedingly castrating. My mother and sister weep in the background, and I am struck.

Max flicks him under the nose.

Ow! That hurt. How did you learn to do it? *He has a nose-bleed.* You see the technique? My father struck me, and now my son . . . My nose! Oh, I'm bleeding! Give me something! Someone! A rag! Ice! Let me smell vinegar! Bella . . . I'm bleeding. I'm undone!

Bella gives him a handkerchief. He collapses in barber chair.

MADGE: Just as things were going good. Take the camera off him.

MOTT: Somebody—do something.

AUFSCHNITT, *in the center of the stage, stunned, frightened as the camera turns on him*: Ladies and gentlemen, my name is Gerald Aufschnitt. I was born in Vienna, also the home of Mr. Freud. I am now Mr. Bummidge's tailor for thirty years. What a wonderful person. He helps me with my troubles. My daughter's troubles, too. I make his costumes in my little shop on Columbus Avenue. He asked me to play in his show. I was just man, in the grip of relentless suppressions. I was never in a show before. How do I look?

MADGE: It's a fiasco. Wink, get on camera.

WINKLEMAN: Good evening. Yes, we are relatives. Were

playmates. My cousin is a man of genius. Without him, my life would have been very empty. It is becoming rare for any person to need any other specific person. I mean, usually, if death removes the one before you, you can always get another. And if you die, it might be much the same to the rest. The parts are interchangeable. But Bummidge is *needed*. . . .

MADGE: Get off with that stuff.

MAX: Pamela! Dance—bumps, grinds—anything!

> *Bertram is now before the camera.*

BERTRAM: By profession I was a zoologist, but got into the exterminating business. For every one of us, there is a rat. One to one. We seldom realize that rats are part of civilization. Rats came from Europe. They couldn't cross the continent until there was enough garbage from the covered wagons. They were pioneers, too. Mr. Bummidge understands. He has taken me on for training and study. He feels I tried to overcome my Oedipal problem by becoming father to myself. That is why I am so stern, why the rats are like children to me, and why I do not laugh. Unless tickled.

> *Mott tickles him and Bertram laughs horribly. They push him from the spotlight.*

MADGE: Pamela, take over.

> *Pamela performs, something between modern dance and burlesque.*

BELLA: It's a disaster! This broad will ruin him. I always said it.

BUMMIDGE, *rising from chair*: The bleeding has stopped. Where's the camera? Ladies and gentlemen, a violent father often has terrible effects on a son, if the son idolizes strength. *He goes toward Max but finds himself entangled in the arms and legs of Pamela.* Age twelve. I lose my virginity, as they say. Seduced on the counter of a dairy restaurant by a certain Mrs. Friedmacher. . . . *Extricates himself*: Locked in my bosom, a child, a little child who weeps. But now I am ten. The perils of reality surround the boy. He flirts with death on the fire escape, on the back of the trolley. Disease is trying to infect me. Time waits to consume me. The Id wants to detain me in infancy till I become like an ancient Mongolian idiot, old, wrinkled, yellow. I run and hide, steal, lie, cheat, hate, lust. Thus . . . my pursuit of happiness!

MADGE: Winkie, if he rambles on like this, we're sunk.

BUMMIDGE: And now I ask you to witness a pair of solemn events. At this moment I am yet unborn. We are behind the candy store in Williamsburg. A January night. *Counts on his fingers.* It must have been January. I don't exist. *Covers his eyes.* Oh, blackness, blackness, and frost. The stove is burning. A brass bedstead. And here they are. *Points.* My parents, male and female. Two apparitions. Oh! *He turns away.*

MADGE: When? Papa and Mama! What's he talking! Bummy, there are limits!

VELMA: Of such things the law should prohibit viewing. Even on closed-circuit.

BUMMIDGE—*pushes Madge aside*: My little sister is sleeping. Unaware. And then—*pointing a trembling hand*—my father takes . . . And my mother . . . Oh, no, Mama, no! Pa! Ma! Wait! Hold it! Consider! Oh, don't do this to me. *To the audience*: It's the Primal Scene. Nobody can come between them. The action of Fate. I am being conceived. No, no, no, no, no! Pray, little Philip Bomovitch. Oh, pray! *On his knees*: But it's too late. My number is up! Bang! *Claps hands to head*: I'm doomed now to be born. May God have mercy on my soul—on all our souls.

WINKLEMAN: Brother! Even the old name, Bomovitch.

BUMMIDGE, *rising, before camera*: And now, ladies and gentlemen all . . . I will ask you to observe the projection of another most significant event. I shall try to penetrate the mystery of birth. I do this in the hope of renewal, or rebirth. This is the climax of my method. I invite you to watch a playlet which attempts to bring together the ancient and the avant-garde. *To group*: I have parts for all of you.

WINKLEMAN: Oh, God, now he's a playwright. Meantime, disaster waits for me.

MADGE: I've staked everything on this!

GALLUPPO, *to Max*: You'll get a bill from me, buddy-boy.

IMOGEN: Here are the parts, Mr. Bummidge.

BUMMIDGE: Hand them out.

PAMELA: I thought it was all impulse.

> *A black cloth has been prepared on the sofa, mid-stage. There are holes in this cloth for the heads of the chorus. The company dons the cloth, Imogen assisting, Bummidge supervising.*

MAX: What is this?

BELLA: A Greek chorus?

GALLUPPO: Why am I the Second Voice?

VELMA: I'm no Greek.

Final adjustments of the black cloth are made.

BUMMIDGE: The title of this presentation is "The Upper Depths," or "The Birth of Philip Bomovitch." Ready . . . get set . . . Go. *Lies on the sofa.*

BELLA, *reading*: The babe is in the womb now.

WOMEN: What far-off force presides over this curious particle of matter?

VELMA: O Kronos!

MOTT, *to Technician*: Who the hell is this Kronos?

VELMA: Speak, Tiresias. Speak, holy hermaphrodite. Blind, you know the darkness best. *Continues to smoke her cigar.*

MEN: The cells of the babe divide.

WINKLEMAN: Seeming chaos. A terrible order.

GALLUPPO: Iron. Proteins.

MAX: The swift enzymes. Transistors of flesh.

PAMELA: Matter torn away from other forms of being.

ALL: Will this be nothing but finite, mortal man?

BELLA: His eyes.

MADGE: Tongue.

PAMELA: Genitalia.

VELMA: His liver.

WINKLEMAN: And his nerves.

MAX: And within the soft skull, a soft mass of white cells which will judge the world.

BELLA: O Transfiguration!

ALL: He is being created.

GALLUPPO: Merely to jest? So that other animals may grin?

MAX: But there is no unmetaphysical calling.

PAMELA: And what is the mother doing? Does she go stately through the slums? Is her mind upon the gods? Does she understand what she is carrying?

MADGE: Not she. No thought, no prayer, no wine, no sacrifices. Only herring, potatoes, tea, cards, gossip, newspaper serials. How far is this Daughter of Man from authentic Being.

WINKLEMAN: The unborn Bummidge, afloat in Stygian darkness.

Bummidge floats like an embryo.

ALL: He's folding, unfolding, refolding. Now he's a fish.

Bummidge enacts the fish.

MAX: Dimly he beholds the geologic periods.

GALLUPPO *and* MADGE: The vacant lifeless seas.

BELLA *and* MAX: Things that crawl.

VELMA *and* WINK: The ferns, the lumbering beasts.

MAX: From stone, from brine, sucking the seething power of the sun.

PAMELA: Now appears the backbone.

GALLUPPO: The gills.

WINKLEMAN: He's a reptile.

MADGE: A mammal. Higher. Up the vertebrate tree.

ALL: Up! Up! This thing is evolving into a man.

Bummidge stands.

VELMA: Reason.

WINKLEMAN: Self-regard. Tragic apprehension. Comic knowledge.

BUMMIDGE, *getting back on sofa*: It's great in here. I like it.

BELLA: Blind and dumb, the babe. Sheer happiness—Nirvana!

GALLUPPO: But it can't last. The pains are starting.

ALL: Contractions.

> *Bummidge sits up on sofa. The chorus makes the cloth billow behind him, by degrees more violently.*

WINKLEMAN: Fifteen.

ALL: Ba-ba-ba-baboom!

WINKLEMAN: Ten.

ALL: Ba-ba-ba-baboom!

WINKLEMAN: Eight!

ALL: Ba-ba-ba-baboom!

WINKLEMAN: Four.

ALL: Ba-ba-ba-baboom!

WINKLEMAN: Two.

ALL: Ba-ba-ba-baboom!

The violent swelling of the cloth has put Bummidge on his feet.

BUMMIDGE: Oh, Mother! Our time has come. *Knocks as if on a door*: Mother! *Stamps his foot*: Mother! The bag is broken. *Sharp cry*: Help! I'm grounded in here. Oh, terror, rage, suffocation! This is expulsion. I hear screams. I'd scream, too, if I could breathe. Tante Velma has me by the head, dragging me, dragging me. Take it easy, Tante—I'm choking. Choking. Air, air, give me air. Agony to my lungs! Oxygen! The light is scalding my eyes. *Newborn, with wrinkled blind face and clenched poor hand, he slaps himself on the behind and gives the feeble infant cry*: Eh . . . Ehh! *He squalls like a newborn infant.*

BELLA: It tears your heart to hear that cry.

MAX: A tyrant. Utterly helpless. Absolute from weakness.

PAMELA: They cut the cord.

Bummidge looks about.

WOMEN: So this is the world?

MEN: It is the Kingdom of Necessity.

ALL: *Sein! Dasein! Bewusstsein!*

Imogen presses an inflated balloon to his mouth.

BELLA: The breast. She holds him in her arms.

ALL: Bliss.

BELLA: He breathes. He suckles.

ALL: Bliss.

BUMMIDGE: Where do I end, and where does the world begin? I must be the world myself. I'm it. It's me.

MAX: A little moment of omnipotence.

>*Imogen pulls away the balloon, which is attached to a long string.*

BUMMIDGE: So *that's* the way it is!

WINKLEMAN: Only the first lesson of reality.

BUMMIDGE, *raging*: Give it back!

>*The chorus now reads him a lesson.*

MADGE: Strife.

PAMELA: Disappointment.

BELLA: Loss.

GALLUPPO: Law.

VELMA: Thou shalt not.

MADGE: Thou shalt not covet.

PAMELA: Stifle those horrible needs.

MAX: Bow your head as all mankind must, and submit to your burden.

WINKLEMAN: The war has begun between the instincts of life and the instincts of death.

ALL: *Ave atque vale . . .*

>*With this incantation they go off.*

BUMMIDGE: Oh, my friends. Men, women, brothers, sisters, all . . . *He crawls forward*: You see me now in swaddling clothes. I thought I was born to life, to joy. Not so. I am a sad, vain, tangled thing. I cannot rest in any state. Would it have been better never to be summoned into this world?

Should I pray to cease being? I was born once. Can I be born again from my own empty heart? I am one of certain voices entering the world, and have not spoken as I should. I chose to serve laughter, but the weight of suffering overcame me time and again. As I rose to my unsteady feet—*rises*—I heard the sins of history shouted in the street.

BERTRAM: The *Titanic*, sinking.

AUFSCHNITT: Clemenceau goes to the front.

MOTT: Lenin reaches Finland.

Sound of bells.

BUMMIDGE: Armistice Day, nineteen eighteen. From the abyss of blood, the sirens of peace. I have a vision of bandaged lepers screaming, "Joy, joy!" Twenty million mummy bundles of the dead grin as the child, Philip Bummidge, intuits the condition of man and succumbs for the first time to Humanitis, that dread plague. Being human is too much for flesh and blood. . . .

IMOGEN: He's having one of his attacks.

MAX: Jesus, Pop.

Bummidge sinks into his barber chair, covers himself with the sheet.

What is he doing?

IMOGEN, *before the camera*: Mr. Bummidge foresaw he might be overcome during this broadcast, being a highly emotional man. As his colleagues, Bertram and I are prepared to spell out essential parts of his program.

BERTRAM, *reading*: "The spirit of Gargantua was captured

by totalitarianism. When lampshades are made of human skin, we see that fun is very big in hell."

IMOGEN, *reading*: "Farce follows horror into darkness. Deeper, deeper."

BERTRAM, *reading*: "Sores and harsh pains, despair and death—those raise loud, brutal laughter."

IMOGEN, *reading*: "And what minor follies are there for the comedian to work with? If he tries to be an extremist, he finds the world is far more extreme than he can ever be."

BERTRAM, *reading*: "As the social order extends its monopoly of power, it takes over the fields of fantasy and comedy. It makes all the best jokes."

IMOGEN, *reading*: "Illuminated by Freudian and other studies, Bummidge tries to understand the situation." *With a soft and graceful gesture of her arm, indicates the figure of Bummidge covered by the cloth.*

BERTRAM, *reading*: "For the spirit of man must preserve itself."

IMOGEN, *reading*: "And can preserve itself only upon a higher level than any yet attained."

BERTRAM, *reading*: "Investigators of sleep know that if you keep people from having dreams at night they begin to be crazy."

IMOGEN, *reading*: "And what is true of dreams is true of laughter, too. They come from the same source in the unconscious."

BERTRAM, *reading*: "So wit and comedy have to be recovered. So the social order does not keep the monopoly."

IMOGEN, *reading*: "Therefore Philip Bummidge, with this bag of money, his last savings, intends to buy, from Franklin Kalbfuss, the Trilby Theatre, which he has made into a butcher shop, and establish there a center, an academy or conservatory of comic art based on the latest psychological principles."

BERTRAM, *reading*: "The characters we are so proud of having, the personalities we show off, the conflicts about which we are so serious (little monsters of vanity that we are, fascinated by the dead matter produced by Ego and Superego), these are the materials of the new comedy. To disown the individual altogether is nihilism, which isn't funny at all. But suppose all we fumblers and bumblers, we cranks and creeps and cripples, we proud, sniffing, ragged-assed paupers of heart and soul, sick with every personal vice, rattled, proud, spoiled, and distracted—suppose we look again for the manhood we are born to inherit."

MAX: The Trilby! He's out of his head, completely. I may have to commit him.

BUMMIDGE, *rising*: I shall now die to the old corn. *He begins to parody old routines*: "Do you file your fingernails?" "No, I throw them away."

MAX: He thinks he's back in burlesque.

BUMMIDGE: "Why did the chicken cross the road?" "That was no chicken, Jack, that was my life."

PAMELA, *who has been in the wings, and now enters*: He's flipped.

MADGE, *also coming forward*: His mind was never strong.

BUMMIDGE: "What did the monkey say when he peed on

the cash register?" "This is going to run into money. . . ."
Farewell, old jokes. *Waving his arms*: Fly away, flap-flap, like
clumsy old chickens. I am sinking . . . sinking . . .

> *Bella comes forward, curious, from the wings.*
> *Winkleman follows.*

BELLA: What's happening to him?

WINKLEMAN: He looks as if he's dying. . . . Is he?

PAMELA: I never could be sure of anything, with him.

BUMMIDGE—*crawls into the wardrobe basket*: The dark
night of my soul has begun. Oh, Lazarus, we are brothers.
I die of banality. Lay me in this mirthless tomb, and cover
me with corn. Let me hear the laughter of evil for the last
time. Oh, demons who murder while guffawing, I have suc-
cumbed. *Reaches for the lid of the basket.* Consummatum
est. It is ended. *Shuts the top of the basket. He emerges
seconds later from the back of the wicker wardrobe trunk.*
But I am Lazarus. I was sick unto death, died, and was
buried. Now I await resurrection . . . the word, "Come forth,
Lazarus." . . . *He waits.* Will no one speak? *Waits.* No one?
Faintly, appealing: Someone has got to speak!

IMOGEN, *timidly raising her hand like a schoolgirl*: Come
forth, Lazarus.

> *Bummidge rises slowly.*

BERTRAM: He's being reborn.

BELLA, *bossy, but stirred as well*: Come forth . . . okay
already, come forth!

> *They break into Handel's "Hallelujah Chorus" and*
> *modulate into the anthem "America the Beautiful."*

Winkleman brings in an American flag. Bummidge is raised to the top of the wardrobe trunk.

MOTT: Cut . . . time. Time. Cut.

IMOGEN: He kept talking about the Last Analysis. Now I know what he meant. Mr. Bummidge! He's white, fainting. Help!

WINKLEMAN: I'll change and be back immediately. *Exit.*

MOTT: What sense of timing! Better than a clock. The broadcast is over.

PAMELA: I have to get out of this costume. Bert, lend me that dress. And I want my diamonds back. Who has them?

MAX, *bending over him*: What's the matter, Dad, is it for real?

BELLA: He's out cold. Emotion really overcame him. Loosen his collar.

TECHNICIAN: Well, that's it. Save the lights. Wrap it up.

BERTRAM: Louie and I will put Bummidge to bed.

> *They carry him out. Pamela follows, unbuttoning Bertram's dress from back.*

MAX—*hurries to telephone*: I've got to see if my deal is still on.

MADGE: No. We're waiting for Fiddleman to call.

> *She and Max pull at the phone. The wire is torn loose.*

See what you've done! It's disconnected.

MAX: I? You did it!

MADGE: All these preparations. All these shenanigans, and you have to eff it all up. How will Fiddleman reach us?

IMOGEN: And Doctor Ratzenhofer, Doctor Gumplovitch. Mr. Bummidge will be very upset.

MAX: I'll run down, make my call, and phone a repairman. *Exit.*

BELLA: It was a fiasco anyway. Pathetic Bummy's always been. It's his charm—boorish and touching, also. But who could take this seriously?

IMOGEN: I have to tell him what's happening, as soon as he comes out of it. *Exit.*

MADGE: Bella, I'm bound to agree. And it's a sad, dismal day for me, too. I don't know what we'll do.

BELLA: I know, you hoped to hush up the scandal. That would take dough. But why did you starve those old people?

MADGE: It was Aunt Velma, chiseling. Malnutrition! I didn't know it was that bad. Handling the aged is a hell of a problem.

BELLA: I'd throw you and Winkie to them. Let them prod you to death with crutches and canes.

MADGE: Bella, help. We'll cut you in. You're a business woman. Handled right, this is a really profitable racket.

BELLA: I wouldn't have the heart for it, it's too sordid. . . . Make me a proposition.

MADGE: We have to move fast. There's an inspector who threatens to leak the story to the papers.

BELLA: Throw Aunt Velma to the wolves. Let her take the rap. A year in jail is just what she needs.

MADGE: No, Winkie is sentimental about his mother. . . . Anyway, I agree Bummy washed out. Fiddleman could *never* go for this stuff.

Police sirens are heard.

What is that?

BELLA: Sounds to me like the cops.

MADGE: Bella, whom do you suppose they want? Us?

BELLA: Get a grip on yourself. . . . What a chunk of money he blew on this today.

Enter Winkleman in his own clothing.

WINKLEMAN: The police are making a terrible racket in the street. Has anyone telephoned?

MADGE: Max tore the wires out. I thought he was going to strike me. Today I wouldn't have minded so much.

BELLA: Winkleman, you know as well as I do Bummy's performance was a bomb.

WINKLEMAN: Ripped out the phone, you say! Fiddleman did send a wire, but that was early. I agree—that broadcast must have emptied the Waldorf. A man of genius turned into a crank is a painful sight. So foolish. And what is his big idea? The Trilby Theatre! So figmentary, improbable, Utopian. I really can't stand these Utopians. I could be sorry for him if I wasn't in such a mess myself.

Enter Fiddleman, the great impresario.

MADGE: Fiddleman!

FIDDLEMAN: I'm here with a police escort.

WINKLEMAN: Now don't be sore, Mr. Fiddleman, we meant it for the best.

BELLA: What are you doing here, Leslie?

FIDDLEMAN: What are you asking? Didn't Winkleman get my wire? I'm here because of Bummy.

WINKLEMAN: Accept my apologies. We had no idea he was so twisted in his mind.

MADGE: Those insane theories.

FIDDLEMAN: What are you talking! I couldn't get you on the phone. He was a sensation!

MADGE: Please, Mr. Fiddleman, don't put us on.

WINKLEMAN: We admit it was a mistake. We're crushed already. Then why punish us with bitter jokes?

FIDDLEMAN: Would I waste time on jokes? This is no joke. He wowed everybody!

BELLA: I can't believe it. From here it looked like a monstrosity. But that's because we're not artists. Bummy is one, so the thing had form.

MADGE: So that's what happened. *Incredulous, then brightening*: Winkie.

WINKLEMAN: It worked. I'm vindicated. We're still with it. He'll pull us out of the ditch. *Lays about with an imaginary whip*. Pull, dammit, pull!

MADGE: We are saved!

WINKLEMAN: I'll go and fetch him.

MADGE: No, wait.

WINKLEMAN: Yes! Bide our time until we figure out the best way to handle this.

MADGE: How?

WINKLEMAN: I'm thinking. My heart is kicking like a child in the womb. Just because you're corrupt is no reason to quit. I know that now.

FIDDLEMAN: You know I was skeptical. Bummy? A has-been, a waste of time. But everybody was floored by him. The scientists? Don't even ask. And the show-business people, their mouths dropped open. Personally, the fellow just stormed my heart—right here. But what's with your phone? I got a squad-car escort from the police department.

BELLA: Tell us how it came over.

FIDDLEMAN: Beautiful. And the whole Waldorf was in those rooms. Everybody in New York, from caveman to egghead. What excitement! Since Valentino's funeral, I haven't seen such a spontaneous mob. Women kissed the television screens. And strangers were hugging and dancing. They wept with laughter, or else they grinned as they were sobbing— sometimes it's hard to tell. The place was like the deck of the *Titanic*.

BELLA: How could we doubt him? But it's like being in the orchestra. You play oompa-oompa-oompa, but out front it's Beethoven.

MADGE: Winkleman, are you thinking?

WINKLEMAN: I am. With all my might I am!

FIDDLEMAN: And when he was born, people were like fish in a net. Stripers, flounders, lobsters—gasping.

MADGE: What kind of money is there in it?

BELLA: Let Leslie finish.

FIDDLEMAN: Some of the toughest crooks in the industry broke up when he said that about being born from an empty heart. They started gushing tears. In a way it was repulsive.

WINKLEMAN: From excess to excess.

FIDDLEMAN: Anyway, the networks, the public, the nation, the American people—they're all his. Where is Bummy?

BELLA: Resting.

> *Enter Messenger.*

MESSENGER: I'm back.

BELLA: I'll take that wire.

WINKLEMAN: I'm his lawyer.

MADGE:—His agent. Give it here. *Opens.* It's signed Kalbfuss.

> *Winkleman drops a coin in the Messenger's hat. Exit Messenger.*

BELLA: Kalbfuss. The butcher who rents the old Trilby property.

FIDDLEMAN: What was that they said about the Trilby, that sagging old joint? It goes back to the Civil War. They used to have boxes with fruits and fiddles on their bellies, like marzipan.

WINKLEMAN: Forget it. . . . Madge, what does the butcher say? Maybe he'll kill the deal.

MADGE, *reading*: "Master, I did not know you were a great genius. Will give lease to property on your terms. A shrine. Should be preserved."

BELLA: He doesn't want it preserved but reopened as a theatre of the soul.

FIDDLEMAN, *loudly*: For Christ sakes! *Softening his tone*: What kind of *shtuss* is this from a woman like you, Bella?

BELLA: I'm just repeating what he said. You heard him. A theatre of the soul. People will come up from the audience and Bummy will work with them. They will act out pieces of life. Bummy thinks a man's character is a lot of old junk—rusty bedsprings, busted axles. We should stop carrying all this ridiculous scrap metal around, we—

FIDDLEMAN: Don't get all wound up. What's he going to run at the Trilby, a sanatorium?

MADGE: I pictured a mental spa.

WINKLEMAN: Is that the whole wire?

MADGE: There's more. *Reads*: "May I be allowed to work with you? My only wish. A man of blood. Living from dead beasts. Who wishes to be redeemed." Signed "Franklin Kalbfuss."

FIDDLEMAN: You see how he moves the people? A butcher! A lousy butcher!

BELLA: Everybody waiting, waiting, waiting for emotional truth. For even a little sign.

WINKLEMAN: And can recognize it only in absurd form. Now, Fiddleman, we have to move fast. You must have some ideas.

FIDDLEMAN: A hundred million dollars' worth.

Enter Bertram, carrying covered dishes.

BELLA: How's Bummy?

BERTRAM: Reviving. Breathing hard, but coming around.

FIDDLEMAN: Who's this?

BERTRAM: I prepared a little spread for after the broadcast. Chopped liver. With my own hands. Try some.

BELLA: Never!

FIDDLEMAN: I already got proposals, option checks. Sponsors were there. Here's one from King Cigarettes—two hundred and fifty grand. Chicken feed. Here's from Imperial Deodorants, half a million.

MADGE: Against what? Give it here.

WINKLEMAN: Let me see this.

BELLA: You must have something in mind, Leslie.

FIDDLEMAN: Of course, I saw it like a flash. Have him do his psychotherapy on TV with famous people—Casey Stengel, Marlon Brando, Artie Shaw.

WINKLEMAN: We'll be smart this time. Incorporate. Put everybody on the payroll. The company will buy real estate to take advantage of depreciation. . . .

BELLA: You'll sell him your lousy old-people's home and get

out of the hole yourself. That's an inspiration straight from the sewer. How can you do it to him?

MADGE: Bella, be serious. This is a business discussion.

Enter Bummidge, led by Imogen; Mott, Pamela, and Max drift in soon after.

BUMMIDGE: Imogen, I feel very vague . . . awfully peculiar.

FIDDLEMAN, *confronting him*: Bummy, look. Who is this? *I* am here in *your* house. Do you know what it means?

BUMMIDGE, *shaking his head*: No. I don't understand.

WINKLEMAN: Come off it! Leslie Fiddleman!

BELLA: Bummy, you were right, and you only.

WINKLEMAN: Not he only. I said he'd make this comeback.

MAX: Comeback? I thought it was a bomb.

MADGE: No. It worked. See for yourself. Here's Fiddleman.

MOTT: So that's why the limousine is downstairs, and the cops, and the big crowd. Bummy, do you hear? We won the sweepstakes! *To Fiddleman*: How was the reception? I must have sent a terrific picture.

PAMELA: Oh, lover, I'm so happy for you.

BELLA: We could have been the greatest family in America, on the cover of *Time,* if only the whores let him alone.

MAX: Pop doesn't seem to get it.

PAMELA: The broadcast was a smash.

IMOGEN: What about the scientific reaction?

FIDDLEMAN: There are about fifty of those longhaired guys trying to get in. I asked the cops to hold 'em back awhile.

IMOGEN: That isn't fair! It was all meant for them.

MAX: We've got business. Keep 'em out. Let the family settle first.

BERTRAM: Bummy, you do look strange.

BUMMIDGE: The grave . . .

MOTT: What does he mean?

BERTRAM: He's referring to Lazarus.

BUMMIDGE: I still feel deathy. I feel both old and new.

MADGE: You stunned everybody.

PAMELA: No more living in filth. What a future lies before us!

> *Bummidge eyes her strangely; he seems far removed from them all.*

FIDDLEMAN: Bummy, what's with the fish eye? Am I a stranger? We've known each other forty years.

BUMMIDGE: Is that so? *Curiously distant*: If you say so.

FIDDLEMAN: Of course I say. Since Boys High, on the gymnastic team. You got amnesia?

BUMMIDGE: All that was familiar is strange, and the strange is familiar. Life and death are two slopes under me. I can look down one side or the other. What was I before?

MADGE: Before, during, and after—a buffoon! Bummy dear, please don't fool around. There's so much at stake.

BUMMIDGE: A buffoon! Oh, how unfortunate. Forcing laughs, you mean? Sucking up to the paying public? Oh, my!

MAX: Now, Father! Are you serious?

BELLA: Yes, what is this, Bummy? Are you pulling something?

FIDDLEMAN: What's with him?

IMOGEN: He's gone through rebirth. He may not be the same person now.

BUMMIDGE, *mysteriously remote*: That . . . is the truth.

MADGE: Let's see if he'll deny his own sister.

MAX: Or me.

WINKLEMAN: Let me handle it.

    All close in about Bummidge.

BUMMIDGE: Please—please don't crowd. Oh, don't touch! It makes me cold in the bowels. I feel you breathing on me. See how my skin is wincing. *He shrinks, draws up his shoulders, warms hands between his thighs.*

BERTRAM: Step back, step back here. Give him air.

PAMELA, *to Bertram*: Hands off! *To Bummidge*: You always liked me to touch you.

FIDDLEMAN: What is he? Putting us on?

MAX: He's trying to get away with something.

IMOGEN: Oh, what an unfair accusation.

BUMMIDGE: I'm not the person I was. Something has happened.

MOTT: Like what?

BUMMIDGE: I am drenched with new meaning. Wrapped in new mystery.

MAX: Oh, can it, Pop!

BUMMIDGE: Pop? *He is mildly curious.*

MADGE: Well, who are you?

BUMMIDGE: I'm waiting to find out. Chaos swallowed me up, now I am just coming out again.

MOTT: That sounds just great. You can use it in a show. Say, Mr. Fiddleman—anything specific?

WINKLEMAN, *showing him the checks*: A little option money.

MAX: Real dough? Let's see.

PAMELA: Show me those.

BELLA: Come on, Bummy—*you* know what's happening. The networks want you back.

IMOGEN—*she has found the butcher's wire*: A telegram came from Mr. Kalbfuss. He offers you the Trilby.

BUMMIDGE—*we can't be sure how much he understands*: The Trilby?

FIDDLEMAN: The old vaudeville dump where you used to perform. You said you wanted it back as a theatre of the soul, or something.

BUMMIDGE: Of the soul . . . I don't know what you're doing here. I wish you'd all go. I feel life drifting into me. Drift, drift. *Laves his bosom with air.*

MAX: He wants to drive us nuts!

IMOGEN: Don't you understand? He's been transfigured.

MADGE: As a school kid he'd pretend to be blind. He'd stare right through you and he'd stagger around. A whole week he made me feed him with a spoon.

BUMMIDGE: I have attained rebirth. I am in a pure condition which cannot be exploited. Noli me tangere. Noli, noli, noli . . .

FIDDLEMAN, *to others*: Can you guess how much my time is worth? Come on. A figure. Five hundred an hour? Ha! Guess again. I can't stick around here.

BUMMIDGE: I am not certain who I am. . . .

BELLA: We'll tell you. We'll straighten you out. Don't you worry, kid.

BUMMIDGE: Oh, fallen man, as you lie suffering in the profane, longing for what is absolutely real . . .

WINKLEMAN: Now he's a sage. I think I get it. You don't know who you are?

BUMMIDGE: But I do know who I am *not*. How many of you can say that?

PAMELA: Bummy, I am Pamela who loves you heart and soul.

BUMMIDGE, *viewing her*: Souls? Hearts? You?

PAMELA: How can you pretend not to know me?

BUMMIDGE: Pretend? *To Imogen*: Imogen, take a note. Write, "Weeping is the mother of music."

IMOGEN, *writing*: Yes, Mr. Bummidge.

MOTT: For God's sake!

FIDDLEMAN: He thinks he'll bring me to my knees. Not these knees. Never.

PAMELA: Maybe I deserve to be treated like this. All I know is I love you.

BUMMIDGE: A note, Imogen, a note: "Is pleasure the true object of desire? This may be the great modern error. We will revise Freud some more—respectfully."

PAMELA: Please look at me, dearest Bummy.

BUMMIDGE: I can't see clearly. It's like I have drops of argyrol in my eyes.

PAMELA: Look.

BUMMIDGE: I'll try.

PAMELA: What do you see?

BUMMIDGE: I'm not sure.

PAMELA: I want you to see me, dearest.

BUMMIDGE: Ah, yes.

PAMELA, *trying to control her vexation*: Yes what?

BUMMIDGE: Yes, of course.

PAMELA: What do you see?

BUMMIDGE: A bed. A king-sized bed. And a photograph on the wall. Is it a graduation picture? Is it an ikon?

PAMELA: Darling, a picture of *you!*

BUMMIDGE: Oh, I know who *you* are. You are the desire I tried very hard to have. How do you do?

PAMELA: Our love!

BUMMIDGE: "Love," but not right. Love, sweet but grimy. Like—I have it. Like eating ice cream from a coal scuttle.

PAMELA: You break my heart, Bummy!

BUMMIDGE: Imogen, a note: "Wouldn't it be better to have a rutting season? Once a year, but the real thing? When the willows turn yellow in March? But only animals are innocent." *To Pamela*: O phantom of erections past, farewell! Bertram, show this lady out. *He takes the bracelet from Mott's pocket and puts it in Pamela's hand.*

PAMELA: I won't go. *She resists Bertram and remains.*

BELLA: I don't blame you, Bummy. It's high time, too. You don't know her, that's right. But you damn well know me.

BUMMIDGE: I faintly recall . . .

BELLA: The devotion of a wife.

BUMMIDGE: Something unpleasant. Like noisy supervision. Like suffocation for my own good. No, like West Point with a marriage license.

BELLA: What do you mean, West Point!

BUMMIDGE: "A-tten-shun! Inspec-shun! Let's see your nails. Your necktie. Your cuffs. Your heels. Your handkerchief. Lipstick? Where have you been? What did you do? Open your fly—hup-two-three-four. The greatest in America!" Bertram, will you escort this lady to the street?

BELLA: Put a rat-catching hand on me and I'll kick you in the head. *She remains.*

MAX: And what about me?

BUMMIDGE: You? I am newborn. . . .

MAX: Aren't you a little infantile for a father?

BUMMIDGE: Aren't you a little old to be still a son? *To Winkleman*: I seem to remember you.

WINKLEMAN: You should. I made you great. And I'll make you greater than ever. I'll put you back to work. Because you've made a new discovery. And you have no time to think of the administration, Bummy. You're too creative. Leave it all to me. Please! Be sensible, I beg you.

BUMMIDGE: I definitely remember you. You make linoleum out of roses. You walk over my soul with gritty shoes. Yes, and you have a strange tic. You tell false falsehoods.

BELLA: Some rose!

BUMMIDGE: I may not be the bud of a flower, but neither am I an old rubber plant. *To Madge*: And you, Madam . . . I believe we once played cards together. You got into the habit of cheating, and you cheated and you cheated and you cheated. . . . A note, Imogen.

IMOGEN: Ready, Mr. Bummidge.

BUMMIDGE: "How does the lonely cactus thrive in deserts dry."

MOTT: Bummy, have you flipped?

BUMMIDGE: "It has a mystery to guard. Otherwise, why stand in the sun—why buck the drought, why live with vultures and tarantulas?"

FIDDLEMAN: And me, Fiddleman?

BUMMIDGE, *hand to brow*: Pardon?

FIDDLEMAN: Where are those damn checks—give 'em here. *Snatches them from Pamela and Mott and thrusts them on Bummidge.*

BUMMIDGE, *examining them*: Are these yours? I don't want them. Imogen, what I want to know is, where are my colleagues? Where are Doctors Gumplovitch and Ratzenhofer and the others?

IMOGEN: Trying to get up to see you. The police are holding them back.

BUMMIDGE: Police? . . . A note: "They say that tragedy makes us look better and comedy worse than we are. But that is puzzling. In the first place, what are we? And in the second place, what is worse?"

WINKLEMAN: Bummy wants to dump his friends, to try to make it as an intellectual. Yes, he's aiming very high. He wants power. Oh, cousin, look out. You'll shoot yourself in the foot. You shouldn't turn your back on us. In spite of everything, we love you.

BERTRAM: Isn't anybody going to taste my liver?

FIDDLEMAN: All right, Bummy. You've had your fun with me. I am shivering with insults. But okay. Now talk turkey. Those checks are nothing. We'll make millions. You'll be the biggest thing that ever hit the channels. A giant, a healer, a prophet. The man who went down into the hell of modern life and took comedy by the hand and brought it back again to every living room and bar in America. You want the old Trilby? I'll fix it for you. Sumptuous. New everything. Gold urinals, if you like. With the most advanced television equipment, and every night capacity houses.

BUMMIDGE: You make me recall the life I once agreed to live. All that I used to do, when only wind and fury could make flimsy things succeed. With forced breath and tired nerves. And an audience smelling like a swamp of martinis and half-digested steak. Well, of course it earned millions. *Looks at checks again.* The world *is* hard up for original inventions.

BERTRAM: Emerson, or was it Elbert Hubbard, said if you invented a better rat trap the world would beat a path to your door.

BUMMIDGE: Or you will be sucked out of your doorway, deep into the boundless universe, as by a vacuum cleaner. So—*to Fiddleman*—as Aristotle said . . .

WINKLEMAN: My God—Madge, I think it's hopeless!

BUMMIDGE: As Aristotle said . . .

WINKLEMAN: Wait, you're overexcited. Sit down. I'll handle it. *Helplessly*: Aristotle . . .

BUMMIDGE: As *he* said, get out of here! *Tears up checks.* Beat it, the whole gang of you.

MOTT: What?

MAX: No, Father. . . .

MADGE: Are you crazy?

WINKLEMAN: I can't desert you. Abuse me all you like, but I'm too loyal.

BUMMIDGE: Without me you are ruined.

MADGE: Yes, and me. Your sister, I'm losing everything.

BUMMIDGE: Bertram, Bertram, throw them all out.

ALL: No. Keep your hands off. I've got old files. I'll sue.

BUMMIDGE: You compel me to take measures? You refuse to let me be? Bertram, the net.

BERTRAM: Right!

BELLA: What's happening—what is this?

> *A device appears above. Bella, Pamela, Winkleman, Mott, Madge, Fiddleman, and Max stare up.*

WINKLEMAN: A net! Duck! Look out!

> *All are caught in the net. Bertram runs up like the ratcatcher he is to see what he has trapped.*

BUMMIDGE, *dancing about in excitement*: Out, out! Drag 'em out!

BELLA: You lunatic!

MADGE: He's going to kill us!

IMOGEN: Don't hurt them, Mr. Bummidge, don't hurt them.

WINKLEMAN: Don't destroy a lifelong relationship.

BUMMIDGE: You came between me and my soul. Drag 'em away, Bertram. *Jubilant*: Oh, I can't bear to see them suffering. Ha, ha! They break my heart, throw them out.

FIDDLEMAN: I'll bring an action.

PAMELA: Oh, help me!

> *Bertram and Bummidge drag all in the net through the doorway. Bummidge slams the door, and then does a dance with Imogen.*

BUMMIDGE: A new life. A new man. I really am reborn. *Sprinkles water on his head from water jug.* I baptize myself.

Bertram enters from other side.

BERTRAM: It worked. Technically perfect.

BUMMIDGE: Just perfect. I could vault over clouds.

BERTRAM, *looking down at scraps of paper*: You tore up nearly a million bucks.

IMOGEN: It had to be done. Bertram, you know it.

BUMMIDGE: No, no, Imogen. I wanted to do it. I did it of my own free will. *Thinking*: Or did those people force freedom on me? Now, where is the butcher's telegram? We have things to do. Work, work! Onwards, to the Trilby. We have to tear up the floors and purge the smell of blood. Go, Imogen, and let in my scientific colleagues. They've been waiting. I will put on my toga. The Trilby will be run like Plato's academy. *Puts on toga, arranges folds.* The Bummidge Institute of Nonsense. We deserve a modern skyscraper like the United Nations, but the poor, the sad, the bored and tedious of the earth will trust us better for beginning so humbly. And we will train people in the Method and send them as missionaries to England, to Germany, to all those bleak and sadistic countries. I am so moved! What a struggle I've had. It took me so long to get through the brutal stage of life. And when I was through with it, the mediocre stage was waiting for me. And now that's done with, and I am ready for the sublime. *He raises his arms in a great gesture.*

CURTAIN